MOSTLY SHORT STORIES

MOSTLY SHORT STORIES

Richard Gibbs

iUniverse, Inc.
New York   Bloomington

"The Budding Artist And The Cherry Tree" was published in 2006 in "The Writer's Circle at The Kravis Center" in Palm Beach, Florida.

iUniverse books may be ordered through booksellers or by contacting:

iUniverse
1663 Liberty Drive
Bloomington, IN 47403
www.iuniverse.com
1-800-Authors (1-800-288-4677)

ISBN: 978-1-4502-1410-0 (sc)
ISBN: 978-1-4502-1411-7 (dj)
ISBN: 978-1-4502-1412-4 (ebk)

Printed in the United States of America

iUniverse rev. date: 05/12/2010

Acknowledgements

I thank my wife, Ilene, and my daughter, Jackie, for reading and rereading all the stories and making suggestions that always made sense. Bert Lewis, Anne Ilton and Barbara and Jack Eisert played cameo editorial roles.

Foreword

Although most of the stories in this collection are based on my experiences as a parent, a dermatologist and an artist, hidden among the tales are veins of fantasy. In some, fantasy stands tall and fact is barely discernible. In others, fantasy is all. I have illustrated each of the stories, and, in addition, have appended more of my art in a centerfold section that is unrelated to any of the short stories.

When I started to write the book, I soon realized that because I had never had anything published other than dermatological articles and texts, no moron of a publisher would invest even Monopoly money in me. So, I decided to have the book published by iUniverse, a Vanity Press, and give it away to people who have influenced who I am, such as close friends and relatives. Therefore, if you are reading this book, remember, my valuable and esteemed friend or relative, that you are also the person most likely to be responsible for many of the problems I have had in life.

My stories have been concocted by what I have seen in my rear-view mirror after a long journey. They include a lot of my cockamamie ideas about life.

Enjoy! And reflect on your own long journey. It's the most important trip you'll ever take.

Richard Gibbs

Contents

A Christmas Eve Mishap

The accident occurred in Snowflake, Vermont, on a cold Christmas Eve, in 1948. Santa was busy guiding his reindeer south from the North Pole and then schlepping toys down sooty chimneys. Because he had forgotten to use his inhaler, the cold dry weather was aggravating his asthma and he was starting to wheeze. These voyages were getting tough. I'm too old for this nonsense, he thought.

Santa also knew that he had to lose weight, but the Whitman samplers were too tempting. Nobody watched him pilfer sweets from incorrectly addressed, undeliverable packages. Once, he almost choked on a nougat filled with caramel and brazil nuts. His gagging roused Prancer and Vixen who just turned their heads sideways, convinced that the sounds were just part of St. Nick's belly rolling and *"Ho. Ho. Ho."* routine.

Another contributing factor to the mishap was that Harry, a reed-thin fireman, lived in a small one-bedroom house with a narrow chimney constructed by a skinflint contractor.

Harry's three kids, Dander, Vicksem and Blintza, shared a sleep sofa in the living room. At night, there were tiny toes nudging nipples, runny noses abutting tushies and bodies crisscrossing over each other. Cuddles, Harry's blond-haired, morbidly obese wife, "shared" his bed, often so sprawled over it that he struggled just to get to the bathroom and take a pee. Getting back was almost impossible. She sometimes flipped him off the bed when she rolled over, so he often slept on the floor.

The household was enlarged by the family's miniature, wire-haired dachshund, Hercules. A tinseled Christmas tree stood in a corner awaiting Santa's visit. The tiny house was barely visible to the approaching entourage because blinding snow was whizzing by horizontally. As the wintry caravan dipped westward, the white clapboard house came into view. Santa exited his sleigh and made his way down the chimney. He was still savoring his last bite of a Christmas log when he realized he was becoming stuck. Jesus. This never happened before. Tiny beads of sweat welled up on his forehead.

The bizarre sounds made by Santa as he became wedged in the chimney reverberated throughout the cottage and made the house shake. It awoke Cuddles first. She wasn't sure, but she could swear she heard muffled sounds emanating from the chimney. "Could that be Santa?" she mumbled to herself. She woke Harry and they tiptoed into the living room, fearing the worst. The kids were now awake and the noise frightened them too. They stared at their parents. They realized that this was no scary TV show that you could turn off. This was the r-real thing!

Everyone was now assembled in the living room, aware that it really was Santa who was stuck. They recognized his white-fur-trimmed boots dangling freely from the bottom of the chimney and saw damaged, gift-wrapped boxes and broken red-stripped peppermint sticks, as well as Santa's silly red hat with its white pompom at its apex, all strewn over the floor. Hercules started to bark.

While Santa's feet were searching desperately for the floor, the kids now started to giggle at the seemingly unattached legs, wriggling to and fro, which also prompted Hercules to bark even louder.

Harry tried to pull Santa down, but to no avail. He stopped and thought for a while. Hm-m-m. He scrunched up his mouth, lifted his chin and, with his eyes partially closed, gazed upward, thinking, thinking of a solution. He pondered the situation as carefully as if he confronted a house on fire. He soon realized that it would be virtually impossible to drag Santa down through the chimney and that pulling him out from above, while simultaneously pushing him up from below, was the solution. But, how? Soon, he concocted a plan.

He bolted outside in his pajamas and searched the sky. Snow was still falling and moonlight was casting spooky bluish-purplish shadows over the white landscape, but he spotted what he was looking for. Santa's reindeers were casually waiting and talking to each other just above the house. Cupid was tilting his head and gesticulating to Comet while pointing his left front leg downward in the direction of the chimney. All the reindeers realized that their boss had a problem.

Harry pointed frantically to the animals and shouted for them to descend to the driveway. Dasher and Dancer noticed him and started to pass the word around. Soon, they were all on the ground. Harry raised and spread out the fingers of his right hand and in a back-and-forth pumping motion, indicating that they should stay put for a few minutes. Rudolph got the message and, with his shiny red nose, signaled everybody, in reindeer language, to wait.

Harry stormed back into the garage, opened the trunk of his car and retrieved a long piece of sturdy rope that he used to tie himself to doorknobs when he entered a burning house. He carefully tied the rope between the reindeer's antlers, ending up with Rudolph. He held onto the free end, hopped into the sleigh and in a deep bass voice, bellowed, "Up everybody. Up." The caravan jolted up abruptly and then curved back above the house with Harry in command. He steered the animals to just above the chimney. All the reindeer aped Harry as he leaned over the side of the sleigh and glanced down at Santa, who, by now, was moving frantically.

Harry lowered the cord, maneuvering it into the chimney and screamed, "Santa. Santa. Grab the cord. Do you hear me? Grab the cord." Santa's arms were raised straight above his head, straining to grasp the rope. He finally grabbed it and jerked it down, almost causing Harry to topple out of the sleigh, reminding him of sleeping with Cuddles.

Santa struggled to say something to his rescuer, but failed because of the chatter of the reindeer who were cheering for the old man. They forced themselves to withstand the awful stress of rope pulling on their antlers. Santa had budged slightly but not enough to dislodge himself.

The family was outside the house now, freezing in their pajamas, but shouting encouragement to Harry. Hercules seemed more excited than anyone. He had never seen reindeer before, especially that odd-looking one with the glowing red-nose. Looking down, Harry, too, had never seen anything like it. The night was clear and the black sky was pimpled with countless twinkling specks. Santa was peeking out from deep in the chimney, still struggling to free himself, while, outside, on the ground, the rest of the family, each jumping up and down, was waving to Harry and cheering him on. The shadows cast from the house onto the snow were eerie, but those cast from the reindeer and the sleigh onto the roof were surreal.

Harry pondered the situation and realized that Santa had to be pushed from below at the same time that he was pulled up from above. Some heavy object was needed to uncork him---something large and strong. Harry had the answer. Bellowing, he outlined his plan to his family and they all immediately scurried into the house. By now, Santa's legs were barely moving and he was starting to feel faint.

As instructed, Cuddles pushed the kids aside and headed for the hearth. She thrust her hands way over her head and grabbed Santa's boots. Harry gave the signal: "One. Two. Three. Now." Synchronously, she pushed as Harry and the reindeer pulled. Nothing budged. St. Nick was really stuck. Fortunately, one of his boots knocked Cuddle's glasses off when she was struggling to free him. She bent over and searched for them. A small gray mouse emerged from the dark of the hearth and scampered across her path. "A-a-a-a-gh." she shrieked, and shot upright, pushing Santa skyward like a cannon ball. Wh-o-s-h. Out popped Santa, still holding onto the rope and plopping into the arms of an astounded Harry. They hugged each other and then pumped their fists high over their heads to celebrate their success. Everybody was clapping as loudly as they could. The reindeer simply shook their antlers wildly and smiled such big smiles that their teeth twinkled brighter than the stars. Santa was teary eyed. He put an arm around his savior and started to reminisce about something that occurred a few years previously.

One Christmas Eve, he had panicked because it took him very long to traverse one family's very tall chimney. He had noticed the chimney's unusual height when he approached the house and realized it would take a long time to descend, but was so preoccupied stuffing jellybeans in his mouth that he totally forgot it. He promised himself that from now on he would always look before he leaped, but as he aged, his memory was beginning to fade.

Santa tried to get the reindeers to land so Harry could get off, but because they were so frightened by their ordeal, they refused. He thought and quickly untied the rope from the reindeer's antlers and tied it to his sleigh. Then he coiled the free end around his hand and fed it to Harry so he could shimmy down to the driveway. When Harry was safely on the ground, the reindeer sailed off into the December night with Santa in full command and an odd, wiggly piece of rope flapping and whipsawing behind him.

Now that Dander, Vicksem and Blintza are older, they can't wait for Christmas Eve to arrive so that can tell their own kids what they saw on that scary but hilarious winter night many years ago. They only wish that Hercules were still alive so they could hear him bark when they retold the story.

A Summer Sandwich

My family rented the second floor of a summerhouse in Belle Harbor on Long Island for five consecutive years, beginning in 1936. We shared the two-story, redbrick house with my Aunt Essie, her husband Harry and their three children. It was always an exciting and hectic summer, particularly suited for an only child. The house never seemed to be quiet except on weekday afternoons when the fathers were in the city working and the rest of us went to the nearby beach. Once, because I had a slight cold, Mom and I decided to stay home. She prepared a lunch that I still remember.

We ate in a back kitchen with sunlight streaming through the two, frilly-white-curtained windows. A brave but overworked General Electric fan did the best it could. There was shiny black linoleum dotted with orange covering the floor. In one corner was the sink with its attached wooden shelf.

Life during those steamy hot summers also depended greatly on the presence of a high, white, two-storied wooden structure known as the icebox. The upper compartment held a crudely hewn block of ice, the lower the food. In the center of the room, was an old oak table with four tapered legs. It was usually covered with a light green tablecloth. Astride the rectangular table, stood six sturdy, yellow wooden chairs with Romanesque backs, horizontally braced with lathing strips.

After all these years, I can still taste a favorite sandwich that I often ate for lunch. Mom loved it as well and was only too happy to prepare it. The bread was fresh, liberally seeded rye. Thinly sliced cow's tongue reclined on a bed of sweetened coleslaw, both covering thick slices of summer tomatoes and a few leaves of iceberg lettuce. A swipe of Russian dressing added international flavor. Wedges of half-sour pickle rimmed the plate. My favorite drink, Pepsi Cola--eleven cavities were found on my initial dental visit!-- filled a tall glass chilled with chipped ice. The fizz was so powerful that it made the inside of my nose tickle.

Mom was in her early thirties. Her tawny-colored, page- boy-style hair hung down covering her ears, suggesting the tendrils of ivy overflowing planters in atria of high-storied Portman hotels. I never liked it. Despite the sad mane, my mother was pretty. She had prominent cheekbones and a small slightly upturned nose with a minute mogul on the bridge. But the money was in her eyes--large, light gray, slightly tinged with cool blue, almost eerie and menacing, but invariably smiling and welcoming. Her lips were banal with just a slight exaggeration of its upper central mass. My mother was always neatly and simply dressed, a conservatism that quietly masked her shapely body, but which was a hallmark of her outlook on things in general. Our conversation drifted but usually returned to my morning's activities or the weather, ordinary stuff, no mention ever made of Hitler and the imminent war in Europe.

I don't eat tongue anymore because of my doctor's obsession with cholesterol, but I have secretly vowed that when I am 80, I will allow myself a yearly addition to my usual monk-like diet. I had thought of celebrating at first with Lindy's famous cheesecake, crowned with those memorable cherries, or maybe even a thick pastrami sandwich, but thinking now of those pleasant summer afternoons with my mother, I know what my first joyous meal will be.

Tit For Tat

In the early morning hours of July, 1940, pinkish-yellow reflected light suddenly brightened the second floor window of a fog-enshrouded, two-story bungalow in Belle Harbor, Long Island. The sound of a car approaching the front of the house broke the silent dawn. The weather was already warm and clammy and ceiling fans had been whirring constantly, laboring to cool my crowded upstairs bedroom.

I had barely slept all night because my mind had been working harder than the fan. I was plotting to trick my teenage cousin, Stan, who still slept innocently in a corner bed. He had done me no harm, nor punctured my thin skin in any obvious way, and the reasons for my villainy were obscure to me at the time. His older brother, Arnie, about 18, was also deep in sleep, two days away from reporting for Army duty at Whitehall Street. Only Terry, their younger sister, tossed a bit, perhaps awakened by my activity. I was their 13-year-old, first cousin and Stan and I, as well as our families, had only known conviviality and joy when we were all together. That is, until that morning.

I dressed stealthily in the semi-darkness, exited quietly into the foyer and descended a flight of stairs. I wavered for just a moment but was undeterred. My treachery had begun.

For two summers, Stan and I had been selling *The Saturday Evening Post,* early on Friday mornings, in front of the town train station. The magazines were delivered to our front door, sometime around daybreak. We hawked the weekly from opposite street corners after arriving with them tied tightly, but piled precariously high, in a wire basket attached to the rear seat of our bicycles. Our goal was to purchase items, such as the Louisville Slugger, which was displayed in the Curtis Publishing Company's catalogue, with the green, Monopoly-sized money we earned from their sale. I can still remember the sweet smell that emanated from the freshly printed magazines.

Although we usually rode our bikes together to the station, on this particular morning, I rode alone and plotted to arrive much before him and peddle my magazines to the blue-collar commuters. I envisioned a windfall of green coupons and the reward of having the wooden bat. My plan succeeded because I arrived moments before the early rush hour and I began selling the magazines almost immediately, although my constant side glances searching for Stan's arrival, probably cost me a few nickels from mismanaging change for my hurrying customers.

About a half hour later, when Stan finally arrived with his own bundle of magazines, I was almost sold out. I thought he'd be pissed, but, surprisingly, his face lacked real anger. As he rode his Columbia across the street to sell his magazines, I could swear I heard a chuckle. As soon as he cut the cord binding his merchandise, he grabbed the top copy, swung it briskly into the air above his head and roared "Saturday Evening Post--just arrived." He then glanced toward me, paused momentarily, and smiled ominously. He appeared to be amused by his younger cousin's actions. He sold few copies. I remember feeling vaguely satisfied at first, but then fearing some sort of diabolical reprisal which kids of our age were capable of devising. Although I didn't realize it when I first hatched the crime, looking back, I recall having a fiercely competitive streak that had just recently surfaced. I sensed its appearance when I played games, like stickball, or when I took exams at school. Because I liked Stan--no, I really loved him--I am still appalled that I had the courage to scheme so. Maybe, treachery was in the air. Germany would soon attack Russia in bold defiance of a peace treaty and the Japanese would attack Pearl Harbor even while their diplomats were conferring in a Washington hotel.

I thought of my actions recently when I read about scientific research that claimed that the brains of teenagers did not fully develop until they reached their mid-twenties. Until then, neural connections crucial to intelligent thinking and reasoning could not be made. Untoward consequences of foolish acts were not immediately registered or understood by the underdeveloped brain. The startling example given to support the researchers' findings was the much longer time needed by teenagers than adults to arrive at a decision when they *considered* the suggestion of scientists that they swallow cockroaches as a lark!

Stan and I rode our bikes home together and joked about my foolish act, but there was something conspiratorial about the way he looked. I sensed that my time was coming.

On Sundays, both families spent the day at the beach, but that day Stan said he might not come to the beach because he wanted to hear a Yankee game on the radio.

Tuna fish or boloney sandwiches were usually prepared and stuffed into a capacious, red tote bag, together with napkins, paper cups and some forks and knives. Slices of pickles were bundled together in wax paper. Frosty cold Pepsi colas were removed from the icebox and joined the sandwiches. In addition, each of us carried a little, cloth gym-bag filled with a towel, a comb, a change of clothing and underwear since we all showered at the public baths under the boardwalk after the day's activities. I had a blue bag with an orange stripe encircling the bottom of it. Stan had a white one. I placed mine on an open shelf to the right of the shower-room entrance before I proceeded to the shore.

I loved the beach, but particularly, the ocean. I was always trying to outdo my cousins with my ability to create as much of a splash and thud as possible when we all dove into oncoming waves. But, I loved building sand castles even more. Terry would usually assist me, but *I* ended up embellishing them with drips of wet sand that were scooped out of the shoreline and allowed to puddle in my right palm and then ooze out of the narrow space between my fingers.

We usually left the beach at about 4:30-5:00 and trekked to the showers. I was generally the most soiled of everybody, wet sand often matting my blond hair, grains of sand residing in my ears, and fanciful designs of the stuff almost camouflaging my reddened arms and legs. I generally showered first before the rest of the family.

When I finished showering, I had scrubbed and wiped off as much sand as was visible. I then walked to the large anteroom of the showering area and retrieved my blue and orange bag. I was stark naked and slightly chilled by an intermittent breeze created by the opening and closing of the bathroom door. I grabbed the bag, opened the zipper and reached for my towel, but I felt not towel, but magazines, stuffed to the brim, bulging here and there and distorting the outer surface of the bag. I became frantic and crazily threw the magazines onto the floor searching for my towel. Several people were in the changing area at the time and they all were staring at this nutty kid, frantically extracting Saturday Evening Posts from his gym bag and flinging them willy-nilly on the wet floor. Naturally, laughter eventually swept over the room.

Son of a bitch! Stan must have arranged his stunt after I placed my bag in the bathhouse, because it weighed a ton and I was not aware of its weight when I carried it to the beach.

None of the family had yet arrived to shower and I was starting to shiver. Just as I felt that I was going to cry, in walks Stan, carrying a white gym bag. The zipper of the bag was already opened and my towel protruded from the top. There was a hint of my *Fruit-of-the-Loom* jockey shorts and my favorite yellow T-shirt peeking out of the same opening.

Stan was laughing uproariously as he approached me, but wasted no time in lovingly wrapping the towel over my shoulders and helping me dry off. We walked home together and I told him I would share my coupons with him.

The U-Turn

Remember the first time you drove the family car without your parents or an instructor? It's something I remember clearly, the way some people recall where they were when Jack Kennedy was shot? It was a Saturday night, just before Christmas, in 1946, right after I had returned home to my parent's apartment in the Bronx. I was on a short school vacation after having just finished four months as a freshman in college.

I had taken my driving test when I was 17 and passed it on the first try, despite some mouth-opening mistakes. I wondered if dad's chitchat with the examiner wasn't influential, since they were both Yankee fans and talked about DiMaggio.

I thought about driving the car again on the train trip home. I was really afraid to drive alone since I had an accident on Fordham Road the previous summer, a few weeks after the test. My father was the hapless passenger. A driver in front of me suddenly stopped short trying to avoid hitting a dog and I slammed into his rear. Dad had to pay to repair the old man's trunk. The sum must have been significant since my father, a generally happy guy, became sullen for several days afterwards. The thought of driving again made me anxious, but that all changed after I took an "Introduction to Psychology" class. Professor Lewis mentioned a study from Switzerland that clearly demonstrated that the quickest way to reduce emotional trauma is to deal with it as soon as you can, the quicker, the better.

I decided to talk about the car, a dark-blue Buick sedan, at dinner when I first came home. The words tumbled out between eating split-pea soup and lamb chops with mint jelly, my favorite meal. Mom was always a patsy when it came to me, but I knew the final decision was in dad's hands. I was an only child, not spoiled, just only, and we were solidly middle class--dad had a second-hand men's clothing store in Manhattan—and my parents seldom denied me anything. On the other hand, I rarely asked for anything. All I needed now and then was some change to buy stamps for my Scott's Stamp Album or the latest issues of Superman, Batman or Classic comics

My father was just starting to eat a piece of cinnamon rugelach and have a cup of coffee.

"Dad," I blurted, "I'd like to take the car Saturday night. I have a date with Dorothy. You remember her--she's Eugene's cousin. In fact, I'm double dating with him. She fixed him up with one of her classmates. We all want to see 'Monsieur Beaucaire' with Bob Hope. It's only playing out in Forest Hills and it's a heck of a trip by train."

My father placed his cup of coffee down and briefly glanced toward mom, then me.

"Well, that's a tough one, Richie. I'm glad you want to put the accident behind you and drive again, but mom and I had planned to see Essie and Harry on Saturday. They're celebrating their twentieth anniversary at the ...what's the name of that restaurant, Augusta?"

"Patricia Murphy's," mom said. "Irving, let him have the car. It may be out of his way, but Harry can pick us up. Why are we always picking him up anyway?"

"Why? You know why. I love driving. And of all the cars I've owned, this Buick tops them all--it drives beautifully. Besides, Harry's really a lousy driver. Aw, why not Richie. Mom's right. Harry can pick us up."

Although I should have been elated, I became a little anxious about driving again. I barely ate dessert. I started to wondered if Eugene and I really wouldn't have been better off just taking the train. The whole thing was giving me a headache. No, I concluded, take the goddamned car and get over your fear.

I hadn't dated Dorothy for long. I liked her but something about her mouth bothered me. It wasn't that she had buckteeth or halitosis or anything like that. It's that when she smiled, she showed a lot of her gums. I had never seen such a gummy mouth. I noticed it most when I told her one of my corny jokes. She was a fabulous audience who made a loud uproarious sound, which began with an odd inspiration whoop that presaged the actual laugh. It was during the whoop phase that her gingiva appeared most prominently. It really bothered me, but her big tits made up for it.

I remember thinking about the car when I was playing basketball outdoors with Eugene the next morning. It was windy and cold and a wayward shot accidentally rebounded off the rim of the basket and caromed over a black wrought-iron fence enclosing the playground. It landed with a thud on the hood of a Ford sedan and almost ricocheted into the hands of an innocent bystander. I kept starring at the car long after the ball was thrown back over the fence, thinking of my date, not with Dorothy, but with the car.

When we finished playing basketball, Eugene said he's come over to my apartment later and we'd get the Buick. When he arrived, I went to answer the doorbell and noticed a note on the table in the foyer. A set of car keys was lying on the note.

"Richie. Here are the keys. Good luck! Mom and I will probably be back before you tonight. Please try to remember to lock the car and turn off the parking lights. Dad."

The car was in front of Moskowitz's grocery. It was parked a little tightly and I visualized a difficult exit. I started the maneuver by backing up a bit and then rotated the wheels counterclockwise. Across the street, a mutt and a white Pekinese, started to bark at each other while their owners struggled to separate them by jerking on their leashes. The dogs were visible to Eugene and I because there was a large empty parking space right in front of them.

As soon as I began my exit, Eugene turned and looked back to be sure no cars were coming.

"Watch out, Richie! Watch out for that car!" he screamed.

I slammed on the breaks. An oncoming car swerved and barely missed hitting my rear bumper. The driver glared at me briefly and gave me the finger as he slowly edged his way down the street.

I knew exactly what I had to do now. I entered the narrow street, drove to the corner, cautiously made a U-turn, and took the empty parking space near the still-barking dogs.

"Eugene. I'm parking the car here. I'm sort of frazzled. Let's walk to the train stop and take the "D" line." He immediately nodded in agreement.

We barely spoke on the trip downtown as our train sped toward 86th Street. The whishing roar in the tunnel and the incessant wobbling of the train made me a little queasy, but Eugene broke my funk with the good news that his father had gotten us two tickets for Sunday's double-header at Yankee Stadium between the Bombers and the Red Sox. As soon as we arrived at our stop, we instinctively dashed for the steps leading to the street, ascending two steps at a time in a rush of competitiveness that always marked our relationship. Naturally, that was my day to lose.

We all loved the movie and the girls loved two of my favorite jokes. It was my distinct impression that Dorothy was less gummy after I aced them all with the punch lines.

Dad asked about the ride the next morning at breakfast. I told him it was a piece of cake and dropped the keys on the table.

"The car's across the street from Moskowitz's. By the way, dad, as you said, it really drives beautifully."

Pond Point

In the spring of 1965, Ilene and I decided to leave New York City and rent a house during July and August. We discussed going to the beach or the mountains. I preferred the sand. Ilene preferred the trees. Being plagued with allergies, I wanted to avoid the tree pollen that triggered my sneezing and coughing. Sand, on the other hand, was Ilene's enemy. Its sneaky way of getting into hair and clothing and its ability to seep between bed sheets and blankets drove her mad. We agreed to try the beach first that summer and the mountains the following summer.

Early one Saturday morning, with the city air changing imperceptibly from cold to tepid, the family set out for Westhampton, a vacation destination of many young couples with kids. Westhampton is the closest of the cluster of small Hampton communities on the south shore of Long Island. The trip took longer than expected due to an unremitting drizzle that caused accidents on the Long-Island Expressway. The road was the major east and westbound artery. It was sclerotic from use by masses of cars and trucks, now almost continually clogging it, and from the dual disintegration of wearied and decades-old asphalt and concrete. The incessant squabbling and bickering of our little backseat passengers plagued the trip. At the height of their arguing, I thought of games that might distract them.

"Watch," I said. " Every time we go beneath an overpass, the radio antenna will go up, and when we leave, it will go down."

The mysterious performance I proposed stimulated them to sit forward in their seats, anticipating magic. My magic consisted of stealthily turning the off-and-on switch beneath the dashboard with my right hand and very carefully using my left hand to steer the car. I moved as far to the right in my seat as I could to conceal the hocus-pocus I prefaced all performances with "Get ready. Here we go," to heighten the effect.

"Wow," the gullible duo exclaimed. "Wow." And then, almost in unison, "How'd you do that, Dad?" I saw them raise their eyebrows, open their eyes wide, and look at each other quizzically. The ruse worked for several years, until one day when there was an accident ahead of me and I lost concentration.

The other really stupid game I played with them during periods when the backseat commotion reached unbearable heights, started when I admonished them, in an excited, loud voice, "OK. OK, no more shouting and fighting. We're going to play *King of Silence.* Whoever talks first, after I say 'Go,' loses." Even now, years after the last game, I am flummoxed by their innocence. Jackie usually lost to her older brother, but not after many unsuccessful attempts to restrain from talking by forcibly tightening her lips. Her maneuvers were accompanied by choking animal sounds emanating from deep within her throat. Eventually she would succumb, laughing explosively, while David would lift his arms in a show of victory. When Jackie won, she was no less demonstrative. No matter who won, within minutes, the calm came to naught because the inexorable Sarajevo was sure to occur and ignite further inane hostilities.

We arrived in Westhampton before noon and looked for Henshel Realty, the agency suggested by a friend. The office was housed in an attractive, yellow-shake building, just off the main road. Dan Eckert, a tall, gray-haired man who ran the office, greeted us. Ilene and I had agreed that we wanted a house with a view in an area with lots of kids. We were willing to spend about $2,500 for the season. Dan suggested that we look at three homes. We all went to his car, but before we all got in, I sensed Sarajevo. David and Jackie had begun opening arguments about who would sit *behind* Daddy in the car. What? What? I sat in the passenger seat with Dan. For some reason, lately, that had become a casus belli between them. David had sat behind me going out, so I suggested, foolishly, that Jackie should sit behind me this time. What a mistake. I should have learned by then not to interfere in their squabbles. David protested shrewdly that the agreement between them was that on all trips, David would sit behind me and Jackie would on the return and since we were not yet returning to Manhattan--I imagined, at that moment, that he would become a lawyer—he should retain his position. Jackie began to cry and refused to enter the car. As usual, Ilene resolved the controversy, by wisely and imaginatively suggesting that, "OK. Jackie could sit in the coveted position in the back seat, but, as *compensation* (and this she emphasized), David could sit behind M-r-E-c-k-e-r-t." I couldn't believe that the lawyer agreed to this. I now wondered if he'd fail the bar exam. As I look back at this absolutely ridiculous episode, it's hard to believe it really happened. Miraculously, everyone followed Ilene's counsel and sat peacefully in their proper seats.

We decided on a house in Pond Point without a view, but with plenty of kids and Jungle Gyms and for a summer rental (Memorial Day through Labor Day) of $2,000. The small bungalow was known locally as *The Cary House* because the author of *Cheaper by the Dozen* owned it. What a great decision! The kids had scores of playmates and Ilene and I became friendly with two of our neighbors, who like us, played tennis at the nearby Westhampton Racquet Club. The following summer, we rented again, but chose a slightly larger house in the same community. Rentals were then about $2,500 for the season. At the end of that summer, Ilene and I realized that it probably was a good idea to buy rather than rent. For $23,000, we bought a one-story, three-bedroom house with a water view.

In 1970, Pond Point was a community of beach homes huddled together north of Dune Road, essentially the only road on the barrier beach of Westhampton's south shore. It was so close to the unpredictable Atlantic Ocean that both the homes and the road were often damaged, even washed out, from occasional hurricanes.

Most of the members of the friendly community were in their thirties or forties, like Ilene and I, and almost all had young kids. The house we bought would become our family's summer home for almost ten years.

A narrow, one-way street branched north from Dune Road and looped through Pond Point, returning to Dune Road further westward. Because there was no through traffic, the area was particularly safe, especially for children, who could roam freely, playing games and riding bicycles from early morning till dusk. And what dusks. Most of the homes had sunset views, and, usually in August, the displays were stunning, consisting of a riot of swirling, pastel colors that marbeled the western skies until the flaming orange yoke slowly dissolved into the horizon.

There were frequent cocktail parties and they often coincided with the sunsets. If the parties were early, kids accompanied their parents. Adults drank scotch on the rocks or martinis and kids drank pop. Laughter and animated chatter always competed with the rhythmic lapping of the bay against the wooden bulk- headings of the houses. Noise from boats barreling through the evening waters speeding hungry mariners home added to the cacophony. Many of the member's dogs lounged lazily here and there, and an occasional high-strung one sometimes stood up and barked at nothing in particular or at firecrackers exploding on July 4th. The ever-present briny air and the laid back atmosphere reminded all of us that, despite the turmoil in the world, we were all in heaven.

By about eight, the parties were usually over, the sky was transformed into a silent, dark-blue canopy and the bay waters calmed. If there were no parties, parents usually reclined on their own chaises while the kids played. Almost everyone barbecued on their deck. The smell of charcoaled chicken or sizzling hamburger patties was usually overcome by the medicinal smell of lighting fluid.

Soon, house lights went on and everyone headed inside. Parents then began the frustrating struggle to convince yawning, exhausted children that it was time to go to bed. On some nights, baby sitters arrived allowing young parents to depart for dinner with friends or a movie in town, but most nights, they just remained at home and either read or watched TV after bedding the kids. Invariably, some family member tended to sunburns or aches and pains accumulated from the day's activities.

The nearby beach, south of Dune Road, was for use by members of The Pond Point Association, membership costing just a few bucks annually. Luckily for parents, every summer, the Association was able to hire teenagers as lifeguards. They perched atop their high, white, wooden chairs usually wearing pith helmets and aviator sunglasses. Zinc oxide camouflaged their noses. Their signature metal whistles were draped around their necks, dangling like amulets over their chests. A few teenage girls usually congregated around the chairs.

The beach was usually crowded with children running, playing ball, digging meaningless holes or constructing fanciful sandcastles, sometimes coated with imaginative drippings of wet sand. Thinking they were wiser, the older ones dug deep protective moats around their structures, but usually to no avail, as the ocean eventually flooded everything in sight, to the uproarious delight of most of the children who started screaming and scattering far and wide. A few were so frightened by the deluge that they would cry and run to nearby parents or mother's helpers for comfort and security. It was easy to spot our kids at their construction sites even though all the children seemed to be blond, blue-eyed and tanned. They almost all had john-john haircuts. Ilene had expensive taste in clothing and the Florence Eisman bathing suits our children wore made their identification a snap.

When the ocean was angry, the shoreline was dotted with teenage surfers, their brightly colored surfboards tossed in all directions by huge waves that were making their final voyage to the shore.

Our gray-shingled house in Pond Point was small, but our deck overlooking the bay was large. Jackie and her friends loved playing on the deck and in the beach grass surrounding it. David preferred riding a bike or playing ball on the narrow road. Sometimes, they both went clamming with friends in the shallow bay waters, but always accompanied by a parent or mother's helper.

Late in July, on a muggy afternoon, an accident occurred while Ilene and I were occupied reading on the deck, irresponsibly oblivious of Jackie and her friends, Ricky and Carole, who were all playing nearby. I happened to be at the house that weekday since I had decided to take the week off. The girls were running and then jumping onto the grass from the barely elevated deck, practicing one of those idiotic games kids play over and over and enjoy so much. Jackie tripped while running, and smashed her face against the ledge of the deck. Abruptly, screaming and crying replaced giggling and laughing. Jackie lay sprawled on the deck, yelling "Mommy! Mommy!" Her face was bloodied, tears were welling up in her eyes, and her hands were grasping her nose. Ricky was frozen, staring at a hysterical Jackie, while sobbing herself and barely able to catch her breath. Everyone was shouting "Jackie!" Carole, crying and trembling, both hands covering her mouth, was standing nearby looking down at my daughter. My memory of the abruptness of the accident, and the vision of my daughter sprawled on the deck, surely injured, maybe seriously, still unnerves me to this day.

As soon as we heard the thud of Jackie's face smash against the wooden deck, Ilene and I rocketed from our chaises. We rushed to her and I realized immediately that she had seriously injured her nose. In no time, neighbors appeared, one suggesting that we call 911 and another running inside our house at Ilene's prompting to gather ice cubes. As I was trying to pry Jackie's hands away from her nose to examine her, the pack of ice cubes arrived. Eventually, I succeeded in removing her hands and saw that the skin around her eyes and nose was darkening. Despite my panic, I remembered that I had a close medical colleague who was an ear, nose, and throat specialist practicing in New York. I told Ilene to apply the ice pack to Jackie's nose, while I ran inside and called him. I was fortunate that he was in and not on vacation. He told me to rush Jackie to his Manhattan office as he was going to run late but would be in his office for a few hours more. I quickly found David and shoved the bewildered 6-year old into our car. Ilene was holding Jackie tightly, sitting in the back with her, attempting to calm her down, but losing it. She was barely able to hold back tears. The family sped to New York, uncertain of what to expect.

Dr. Morris Schwartz, the ENT specialist, told us, after getting an X ray, that Jackie had indeed broken her nose. Surgery would definitely be required to correct it, but not now, as she was too young and still growing. He recommended care and reassured us that she would be fine. For the most part, we were relieved, although the thought of her being operated on was unsettling.

On the way home, Ilene and I discussed the accident. There was not a sound from the peanut gallery. I glanced in my rear view mirror and saw two Kings of Silence, dead to the world.

Ilene and I carried the kids to their beds when we arrived in Pond Point late in the evening and then collapsed into bed, immediately falling asleep. But we awoke in an hour or so. We both had a miserable night tossing and turning, replaying the terrifying day over and over in our minds. In a few days though, things were back to normal except for Jackie's nose, which had a small bump on its bridge.

When I think of August in the Hamptons, I usually don't think of accidents. I think of an early morning swim in the ocean, of a game of tennis at the local club, of joyous times spent playing with the kids near the shoreline and of the taste of freshly picked, sweet corn. We bought the corn at a local farm stand run by a large family that had fresh Long-Island produce.

Near the beginning of the month, we drove there and met next-door neighbors from Pond Point. We had a pleasant chat despite a bored David tugging at Ilene's skirt. While we were chatting, out of the corner of my eyes, I realized that Jackie had busied herself petting a small dog. She loved pets and this one was cute. It was a dark-brown, miniature female dachshund. Its truncated tail was wagging vigorously. Its pink tongue was working Jackie's hand and she loved it, smiling as much as the dog was yapping. David looked on disinterestedly. Because it was rumored that the owners of the stand always had reasonably priced dogs for sale, I knew it was all over. A smiling Ilene glanced my way and saw (I'm sure!) a middle-aged, balding father with a silly grin on his face. My bill for the fruits and vegetables that day was much more than usual, but, as I told our neighbors who stood behind us at the checkout counter, it did include a dog.

We drove home tossing out names for the dachshund. David's suggestion of *Sam* was greeted with an awkward silence. My *Tiny* did no better. None of the many subsequent names seemed acceptable to all until Jackie shouted out *"Choochoo."* The winning name was greeted with cheers and laughter, and the noisy outburst prompted the dog to start barking, giving me pause about our canine addition. *Choochoo* continued to bark all the way home, louder and louder as our hilarity grew.

The time it took to name the dog was long compared to the monikers I invented for my kids. One afternoon, for reasons totally unknown to me, I called Jackie, *Tushie Bender* and would use it with affection from time to time and for years to come. It would always bring a smile to our faces.

I sometimes called David, *"Charlie."* The choice was as enigmatic as Jackie's nickname, but one that occasioned an odd encounter at a pet store near our apartment in the city. David wanted a turtle and the store had several that he liked, so he dickered for quite a while. Out of nowhere, several customers entered the store and the salesman's patience with us began to wear thin.

"Come on *Charlie*," I blurted, in exasperation. "Make up your mind."

Unexpectedly, the salesman chimed in with, "Come on *Charlie*, which turtle do you want?"

It seemed like *Choochoo* was the sole topic of conversation and activity for the next few days. We shopped for the dog, held the dog, talked to the dog and tried to deal with its night music and daytime accidents. It amazed me that this tiny creature could create so much turmoil. I definitely recall taking an earlier train back to my office that Monday morning.

Choochoo turned out, however, to be a font of happiness, but she also brought some unpredictable sadness.

It was obvious to us all that *Choochoo* was Jackie's dog. She schlepped it everywhere she went. She fed it, bathed it and walked it, although Ilene and I took turns walking it after dark. We had purchased a long crimson leash and when Jackie walked *Choochoo*, it literally pulled the four-year old along. Once, it yanked too hard and ran free, its leash flipping wildly behind it. A surprised Jackie bolted after the dog. The incident was not without risk to them both because Pond Point was surrounded by water and neither Jackie nor the dog could swim. Ilene was inside the house preparing lunch and David was watching TV.

Jackie's shouts alerted Ilene, but more importantly, Nick Damato, a neighbor, who was leisurely strolling by. He caught the snaking leash just as the dog neared the bulkheading of a nearby house, a few yards from the bay. But unfortunately, Jackie tripped on a small tricycle and toppled onto the road injuring her nose again. Ilene hurried to Jackie; visual images of the earlier fall were still fresh in her mind. Jackie's nose soon began to swell, erasing her slight nasal bump, and the skin around her eyes and nose was now beginning to discolor. Ilene and Nick brought Jackie into the house. My daughter's hysteria was calmed by the reassuring presence of an unharmed *Choochoo*.

The accident was almost a replica of the one a few weeks prior except that I was absent. Ilene called me at the office and I suggested that she drive Jackie to the local hospital this time because I knew that Morris Schwartz didn't work on Wednesdays. Nick reassured me that Jackie was all right, although hearing her crying in the background, made me wary.

He drove the household to Central Suffolk Hospital's Emergency Room. I cared for my patients and spoke on the phone but was unsteady. Ilene called me from the Emergency room to tell me that X rays were taken, but the doctor wanted to see the previous X rays from Dr. Schwartz because of the history Ilene had given him about Jackie's prior fall. Ilene said the emergency room physician seemed perplexed about something he saw on the X ray. His concern disturbed both of us, but we had no choice other than to await the arrival of the Dr. Schwartz's X rays before we knew the status of Jackie's nose. After we endured a week of barely controllable anxiety, tinged with bouts of depression, Ilene and I were informed by both physicians that Jackie had miraculously straightened out her previous nasal deformity and no surgery would be required! Both men spoke with amazement at the bizarre outcome, but Morris said he had seen it once before.

Ilene and I no longer live in Pond Point. We moved to another area on Dune Road, but we are often reminded of those years--sunsets that take your breath away and that I, as a Sunday painter, know cannot be realized on canvas, views from your deck of boaters coming and going, frequent cocktail parties, and, of course, the beach with the sound of laughing children, and even screaming children, usually because of a fall or because a watery tentacle of the ocean had obliterated their sandcastle.

Buried Alive

After our parents died, Ilene and I inherited scores of photographs of unknown relatives who lived mostly in shtetles in the Ukraine and Poland. Some of the pictures were in cardboard shoeboxes, some were loose and many were in piles secured with desiccated rubber bands. The photographs were stored in a closet, piled pell-mell, high up on a shelf, out of mind and almost out of sight. I never got around to examining them closely because when you're young, who's really interested in such stuff.

Naturally, many photographs were old and frail, like I remembered many of our relatives here in the United States. Whenever I attended family affairs, these strange gray people were always seated together, ghettoized, their faces wrinkled and their shoulders hunched over as they spoke to each other, the men talking in loud voices, the women barely audible. Who were these people? Why did they always seem so alien, so foreign, seldom participating in the frivolity and joy of family affairs? I had noticed that they always ordered fish or chicken, never the thick slabs of steak or roast beef Ilene and I and our cousins ate. They surreptitiously popped pills into their mouths between courses and the men were always going to the john. All of them, almost always, left early.

One morning, before going to work, I was in the closet reaching for a hat that was near the photographs, when one of the packets of pictures toppled over and fell to the floor, scattering relatives all over the place. I gathered up the photographs and was suddenly struck by a somewhat faded, black-and-white picture of an elegantly dressed, pretty young woman. She seemed to be staring directly back at me. It was sort of eerie. For a moment, just a very brief moment, I almost heard her whisper something plaintive. What the hell was going on, I mumbled to myself. I turned the picture over and there, in barely discernible slanted letters, was written, "Rose." Rose who? There was no date affixed, nothing about where the photograph was taken, and no identifying exactly who this woman was, although I immediately thought it was someone from my mother's family. I gathered up my relatives and placed them back on the shelf. Puzzling things frequently happen to all of us. We ponder them briefly and just continue with our over-scheduled lives. These fleeting thoughts are like the swift passage of a bird, almost like life itself, but for some strange reason, this bird was memorable.

A few days later, I was told that my dermatological nurse would not be in because her best friend's father had a fatal heart attack. Like all such dreadful news about strangers, most of us react to it with a bit of anxiety because of our own mortality. Yet, someone had just died, someone who lived a real flesh-and-blood life, like our own, and now was silent forever. I think we jettison this anxiety by reasoning that we never met the departed, never knew anything about them and usually had no idea of what they looked like. But, strangely, that morning, something clicked, and I thought of Rose.

I decided that I was going to investigate all my relatives, silently confined, ignominiously, on the darkened shelf of our bedroom closet. I envisioned that the door of the closet might rattle slightly if I approached it again because of the agitation and excitement my revisit would engender among its residents. I imagined how eager they were to tell me stories about their lives, even their deepest secrets, totally unknown to anybody, even to their spouses. They were probably thinking--what the hell, why not tell him. I'm sure their days and nights were sprinkled with happiness and festered with frustrations, no different, I imagined, than all of our lives today. Except for the Cossacks. And, the

Tzar. And, the pogroms. And, the bitter anti-semitism that permeated all things Russian and Polish in their time.

After dinner that night, I glanced at a few dermatological journals and quickly looked through the mail. I was now ready for the closet thing. I entered the sanctuary, warily glancing at the stuff on the shelf--for a moment it almost seemed to shimmer--took it all down and one by one carefully studied each photograph front and back. I searched for telephone numbers of older relatives in my Rolodex and in phone books. I felt like an adventurer exploring uncharted land.

I hoped my aging relatives were still alive and some were. I called those whose numbers I had and questioned them by shouting into the phone. I got rudimentary genealogical information from several cousins. A few of them gave me names and telephone numbers of other relatives who they thought could help. Because some of them had heard I was a dermatologist, one who knew zilch about the family, questioned me about a tiny pimple on his nose that had started to bleed. One even told me, in endless detail, about a complication from her recent bunion surgery and another asked me about the twitches of a neighbor. An older uncle, Yankel Garfinkle, suffered what I suspected was an epileptic fit while talking to me on the phone. I made some medical suggestions to his hysterical daughter after she grabbed the phone from the old man's trembling hands.

Despite these obstacles, I slowly started to construct a rickety genealogical tree. I got as far back as the end of the 19th century. With persistence and help from my first cousin's wife, I obtained a manifest of "The Rotterdam," the steamer that left Europe on the last day of August in 1912 and arrived in New York ten days later. The manifest listed the Polish town where my mother and her family lived. It listed grandma and grandpa's age as well as the ages of their four children, my mother and her sisters. There were seven children in total and three were left behind in Poland. They subsequently emigrated to New York a few years later.

I was a little surprised at the age of my mother when she arrived. Mom always told me she was born in 1911 and she was one when she arrived in America, but on the manifest, it clearly state that she was eight. I immediately envisioned her as a gray-haired woman with hands covering her face because she had lied, now hiding in an album in my closet, weeping a bit, and wondering why I had intruded on her decades' old sleep and peace.

The time-consuming project was more than I asked for. It lured me away from my other interests. I began to rue the day when the buried beckoned me, but also felt an obligation to do the right thing for my kids and grandchildren. I only wish that as I age and become gray, they will do right for me and read it. I'm already into chicken and fish and, because of a hearing loss, talk loud. Last week, my doctor suggested I take a drug four times a day, but often I forget because I'm distracted by my frequent trips to the john.

The Ingredients Of Love

A cousin's recent divorce prompted me to examine my own marriage in the same way that a friend's disclosure that he has prostate cancer might have prompted me to visit a urologist. It also encouraged me to ponder the success of the marriages of my friends.

Vivian and I have been together for over 45 years. I've often thought of our marriage as rock-solid with minor cracks here and there, but nothing with a Richter rating. When I began to consider the reasons for our bliss, I was surprised that some of the reasons were not obvious when we first met.

Looks have always been important to me and Vivian has always been Ingrid-Bergman pretty. Her common sense, sharp mind and affability were also obvious to me from the start. These traits have contributed to relative harmony within our family and with close friends. They made everything we did together easier. I also know that her intelligence has often helped me avoid unnecessary expenses in more than one financial deal. Sure, we argue, sometimes angrily and loudly, but on the whole, we can engage in civilized discussions of contentious, hot button political and social issues without rancor.

Her father, the General in her family, imbued her with a fondness for mathematics, resulting in her having an idiot savantic recall of almost any number she encounters. For example, how many people instantly remember all their credit card numbers and all the cell phone numbers of friends? She is also a whiz at comparing and remembering the prices of clothing and accessories seen in zillions of shops, a difficult feat, but an existential one, for a marathon shopper like her.

Vivian has uncanny mechanical skills that I didn't recognize at first. Once, she disassembled and reassembled an oven door--yes, an oven door--hours before a dinner party, because the oven was not heating up adequately. She tackled and solved the problem after she uncovered and repaired a slightly misaligned door hinge. See what I mean?

Equally amazing is her ability to resuscitate malfunctioning electronic gadgets, especially television sets, TIVO's and VCR's. She's unsurpassed on basketball nights, since my world, like Steinberg's, starts in mid-town at Madison Square Garden with the New York Knicks, and barely extends westward. How many times over the years have I frantically summoned her to the den to restore clear weather to a snowy TV screen? She first reads any accompanying technical booklets. Knowing me, I certainly wouldn't read them first. I'd try a little zetz here and a little bang there.

Naturally, my attempts usually fail, so I call her. She takes over and starts her detective work. Slowly, she rereads any technical information supplied by the manufacturer. She then busies herself behind the set and supplements her mechanical skills with ceaseless muttering and grumbling that is totally devoid of expletives or curse words. She systematically inspects and tightens every plug and wire and sometimes asks me to get screwdrivers or pliers to aid her. Usually, I'm still in the room to hear her request to fetch the tools, but if a particularly important game is on, I've probably disappeared into the adjacent kitchen, turned on our small radio and fiddled with it until I locate some crummy local station carrying the game. Her repairs are invariably successful, however, and in no time, I'm a happy and contented fan, reclining peacefully in my Barcalounger, stroking my longhaired dachshund, *Time-Out*, with one hand and holding a glass of apple juice with the other.

We have several married friends and their marriages vary widely in success. The first couple that pops into my mind is the Hoppers, Sheldon and Lucy. Their relationship makes Martha and George's in "Who's Afraid of Virginia Wolf?" seem like Ma and Pa Kettles.' The Hoppers argue constantly. Ad hominem attacks seep into all disagreements.

It is enervating to fight with a spouse, but, as Sheldon mentioned last week, it is beyond nightmare, to experience the agita in dreams. Sheldon says he gets little sleep and when he awakens, he is shaking and drenched in sweat. The horror never ends.

Lucy argues with Sheldon about *the* most insignificant and minor things. If he says up, she says down. It seems to him that even if she is wrong, he ends up losing the argument because, as part of her recalcitrance, she is prone to thrust her right index finger into his chest to emphasize some point and sometimes he ends up with tender black and blue marks, or as Lucy corrects him, "blue and black marks."

The persistence of their disagreements once cost Sheldon big time. About a year ago, he was driving Lucy to her psychiatrist in heavy traffic when they had an argument. That was it. That was it. He decided to stop the car and tell her to get out and *walk* to her shrink. But, in pulling over to let her out, he became so distracted that he slammed into a Hummer that was breaking to avoid hitting the car in front of him. Sheldon's new Lexus 430 was totaled and he broke his jaw, requiring extensive surgery to wire it shut and forcing him to spend weeks in the hospital. He dreaded Lucy's hospital visits, because even though he was physically unable to talk, the termagant usually started to recall previous arguments, some from their first date, but most from when they were first engaged. They recently told us that both their families came from Bulgaria and I wondered if they look at things differently there.

I always thought that there was a highly successful marriage between one of Vivian's college roommates, Ida, and Oren Katz, or OK, as we've called him for years. He never refuted anything Ida said, never criticized anything she did, and never complained about her almost inedible meals. They did fight occasionally but only about minor matters. All of his friends considered him a milquetoast, but the Katz' are very much in love and we consider their marriage a success.

Most marriages have stormy periods, but seldom does the *perfect storm* develop. Tranquil periods usually prevail because people usually learn from their mistakes and rectify their behavior to live in some sort of harmony with their spouses. But, every now and then, people marry with little forethought to the obvious consequences and the results are predictable—disastrous!

My old buddy's marriage is a perfect example. Carmello was a divorce lawyer, the scion of a wealthy, real-estate family. He successfully arranged an equitable separation between Edna, a beautiful, red-headed, massage therapist, and her husband, Sidney. Carmello had the hots for Edna from their first meeting. They started going out and, in no time, they contemplated marriage even though Carmello was fully aware that he would become her seventh husband! Undaunted, he jettisoned his wife and married her last week. Vivian and I predict a category-five hurricane accompanied by a Guinness-book-eligible tsunami in a short while, probably on their honeymoon.

Length of marriage or religious compatibility is no indication of success. Just last week, The Daily News reported on the 68-year-old marriage between a 95-year-old religious Jew, Schlomo Nockoff, and his 93-year-old wife, Mindy. Neighbors praised their relationship, but according to their grandson, Sidney, who was visiting on a Sunday morning, an altercation developed between them. Mindy was criticizing Schlomo's table manners. This was nothing new. She also criticized the way he dressed, even the way he peed, wetting everything within three feet of the toilet bowl. Schlomo became enraged. Before the grandson could stop him, Schlomo grabbed a huge bread knife and frantically and repeatedly stabbed Mindy almost to the point where there was no more places to put the knife. The butchering cost Schlomo his life also since he died of a heart attack later the same day. Sidney swears that

Schlomo had a smirk on his face and Mindy an incredulous look on hers shortly after they both died.

So, what are the ingredients that make for a successful and loving marriage? Because there are so many ingredients, it's like a bowl of chicken soup with noodles, served to friends. You start with over a dozen ingredients: water, chicken stock, chicken breasts, butter, noodles, celery, carrots, green beans, salt and pepper, mushrooms and parsley. You make the soup and you serve it. It's not hot enough! Ugh, too salty. Why the Hell did you use so much pepper. You know I get reflex. You call these noodles? They're as hard as watchbands. Now, these are delicious noodles. You know, I'm getting tired of chicken soup. Maybe next time you can make gazpacho? Wow, I always hated celery but it tastes great now. This soup is the best, absolutely the best! Can I have the recipe?

Gallery of Art

First hole. If you are a golfer, have you ever notice that players seem so jovial and in such good humor at the first tee, but lack that happiness after they've finished playing when they become sour and glum.

2005, 30"X 40," acrylic on canvas, collection of the Florida Atlantic University, Lifetime Learning Society on the John D. Mac Arthur campus, Jupiter. Florida.

How's this swing for an 8-year old? My grandson, Grant.

2008, 14"X 11," acrylic on canvas.

Discussing the game.

1995, 20"X 20," acrylic on Masonite board.

Out! Some tennis players have a speech problem. When the ball is hit onto their side, they cannot say "In." I've shown these knuckleheads how I move my lips and tongue so that I can say the word. I've been very patient with them, even offering to pay for a consultation with a well-known speech therapist. No luck! As hard as I try, their call is invariably "out,"once even when I was just starting to serve.

1993, 20"X 20," acrylic on Masonite board.

" ...AND LET'S START REDUCING MRS. PLOTKIN'S CORTISONE."

1961, 6"x9," India ink on Bristol board.

Dermatological meetings. Dermatologists usually meet periodically to discuss patients whose skin disease is either undiagnosed or recalcitrant to therapy. The patients are examined in cubicles. I used to imagine that they sometimes wished that the encircling crowd of busybodies would just go away.

1960, 6"X 12," India ink on Bristol board.

**Sometimes the dermatological discussions
afterwards would get prickly.**

1960, 6"X 12," India ink on Bristol board.

1962, 6" X 9," India ink on Bristol board.

1961, 8" x 5," India ink on Bristol board.

1963, 7" x 8," India ink on Bristol board.

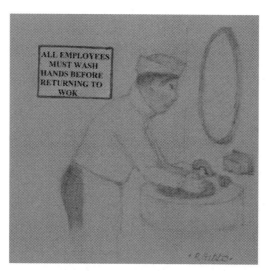

2009, 5" X 6," pencil on Bristol board.

2009, 5" x 4," Pencil on Bristol board.

2009, 4"x 3," India ink on Bristol board

"Why Dr. Schnecker. That's the funniest joke I ever heard."

2009, 6"x 7," India ink on Bristol board.

7" x9," India ink on Bristol board.

"When ol' doc Moses says they have gallstones, you better believe it!"

2009, 6"x9," India ink on Bristol board.

Beach Scene Of Father With Sons.

1995, 14"x 14," acrylic on canvas.

Beach Scene-II. Westhampton Beach.

2005, 30" x 40," acrylic on canvas, collection of Florida Atlantic University,
Lifetime Learning Society, on the John D. Mac Arthur campus, Jupiter. Florida.

Catamaran.

2004, 40" x 30," acrylic on canvas.

Pregnant Woman On The Beach.

1996, 22" x 28," acrylic on canvas.

Inflatable Raft And Surfboards.

2002, 32" x 42," acrylic on canvas, collection of Florida Atlantic University,
Lifetime Learning Society, on the John D. Mac Arthur campus, Jupiter. Florida.

Beach Conversations On A Lazy Sunday Afternoon.

2000, 19" x 19," acrylic on Masonite board.

Three People On The Beach.

2004, 31" x 41," acrylic on canvas, collection of Florida Atlantic University,
Lifetime Learning Society, on the John D. Mac Arthur campus, Jupiter. Florida.

Two Older Women At The Shore.

1990, 16" x 21," acrylic on canvas.

The Yellow Surfboard.

1988, 30" x 40," acrylic on canvas, private collection.

Beach Scene With Old Men.

1991, 16" x 20, acrylic on canvas, collection of Drs. Stanley and Sylvia Epstein.

The Yawn.

1999, 20"x 26," acrylic on canvas.

Beach Scene-I. Westhampton Beach.

1988, 41"x 41, "oil on canvas, , collection of Florida Atlantic University, Lifetime Learning Society, on the John D. Mac Arthur campus, Jupiter. Florida.

Girl Walking Along The Shore
1995, 10" x 8," acrylic on canvas, private collection.

Building Sandcastles-II.
1998, 18"x 24," acrylic on canvas.

Beach Scene-III,
1998, 16" X 20," Oil on canvas. Collection Westchester Cardiology Group.

Dozing Off On The Beach.

2006,16" x 20," acrylic on canvas.

Proud Grandfather.
2000, 10" x 14," acrylic on Birchwood panel.

Pensive Model.
2003, 12"x 16," acrylic on canvas.

**My Dad And I After I Had Just Graduated
From Medical School In 1954.**

2008, 10"x 14," watercolor on Bristol board.

Man Reading Newspaper In Paris Park.
1996, 13"x 10," watercolor on Bristol board, collection of William Applestein.

Winter Scene, Foley Square, New York.

1995, 15"x 19," oil on canvas, collection of The Director's Guild of America.

Christmastime, 34th Street, New York.

1985, 10"x 14," watercolor on Bristol board, collection of the
Skin and Cancer Unit of New York University Langone Medical Center.

Homeless Street Person.

1991, 12" x 14," oil on Birchwood panel.

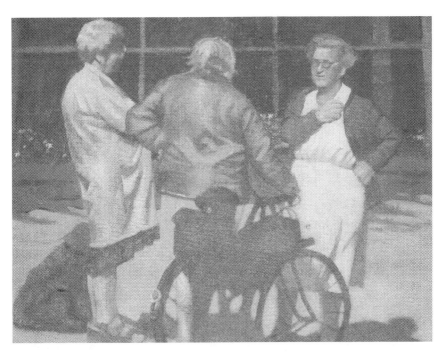

Street Scene, Lathorp, England.
2000, 10"x 13,"acrylic on canvas.

Girl's School Outing In Park In Melbourne, Australia.
2002, 39"x 43," acrylic on canvas.

Carousel In Paris.

1999, 18"x 19," acrylic on Masonite board.

Bus Stop At First Avenue And 34th Street, New York.
1992, 18"x 19," acrylic on canvas.

Students On A Lawn In Paris.

2000, 18"x 30," acrylic on Masonite board.

School Playground, New York City.
2006, 31"x 41," acrylic on canvas.

The Jogger And A Disabled Woman With Her Companion.

2002, 10" x 14," acrylic on canvas.

**Boy Looking At Toys In A Store Window.
As A Kid I Did The Same. Now, I Toy With Stories.**

1990, 14"x 19," acrylic on canvas, private collection.

Fruit Stand In Front Of Grand Central Station In New York.

2004, 30"x 40," Collection Of Florida Atlantic University, Lifetime Learning
Society On The John D. Mac Arthur Campus, Jupiter. Florida.

Morning Park Scene In Paris Of Inscrutable Man With Children And Dogs.

2005, 30"x 40," acrylic on canvas.

Winter Scene-42nd Street And Park Avenue.

1995, 12"x 14," acrylic on canvas.

Con Ed Workmen, New York.

1999, 16"x 20," watercolor on Bristol board.

**Ballet Class, Dallas. My Grand Daughter,
Olivia, Is On The Extreme Right.**

2004, 16" x 20," acrylic on Masonite board.

Fruit Stand In Midtown Manhattan.

1993, 16" x 20," oil on canvas, collection Director's Guild of America.

Old Couple Watching Children Play In Sandbox In Paris Park.
2000, 10"x 14," acrylic on Masonite board.

Thinking-I.

1978, 4,' Marine Styrofoam, concrete, two-part marine epoxy and acrylic paint.

Abstract Figure-I.
1979, 8," Plaster of Paris and Vermiculite.

Nevelsonesque Sculpture.

1980, 12,' x 4,' Plywood, lathing strips, Elmer's glue, and
dermatological, personal and found objects.

Grief.

1983, 7," Water-based clay, Elmer's glue, household epoxy and acrylic paint.

Reclining Nude.
1982, 5," Water-based clay, Elmer's glue, household epoxy and acrylic paint.

Standing Man
1982, 9," Water-based clay, Elmer's glue, household epoxy and acrylic paint.

Conversation On A Bench.

1984, 15"x 10"x 5," Plaster of Paris, cardboard, lathing strips and acrylic paint.

Ten Years Of Aggravation

I've played golf for about 10 years and I'm a basket case. I have tried everything to improve my game; instead, I'm getting worse. Fortunately, I think I've figured out what to do about it.

I have always been a decent athlete, not great, but never the poor slob who was always picked last in baseball or basketball. In fact, when I played tennis, I became an A-player, not bad for a guy who took the game up at forty. I played for about twenty happy years, but had to give it up because of bad knees. At the urging of my friend, Norton, I contacted a young golf pro named Iago, and took up the game.

Sports have always been important to me. Stickball and basketball were my favorite games as a kid, but I also liked baseball and I had a whiz of a chop shot in ping-pong. Sports told me where I stood in life. It gave me some sort of score. Of course, other things told me how I was doing. I was middle class, but I knew rich kids with chauffeurs and fancy apartments. I never envied them, but I vaguely understood that I was an underdog of sorts. Guys who dated chicks with big boobs always put me in my place. My close friend Big Dick, who *scored* on all of his first dates, ranked high in my social hierarchy. When I got older and became bald, guys with hair also ranked high, even if they were lousy at sports.

When Iago started teaching me, I was close to 60, but still quite fit. At the suggestion of golfing friends, I spent a week at a golf camp in Scottsdale, Arizona, trying to familiarize myself with the game. Unfortunately, it was fun.

On the first day of camp, the pros had urged me to loosen my grip, feel the weight of the club and, most important, swing easy. Forget it, I just couldn't. On the third day of camp, I threw my back out and had pain down my right leg because of my belief that the golf swing was like the baseball swing. I was in bed for two days, barely able to walk. My sole consolation was being able to read the piles of golf books and magazines the pros gave me.

In time, my sciatica resolved and I started to play on local public courses. I ripped fairways to shreds with my clubs, because in the beginning, I often missed the ball completely and hit turf. My score was north of 150. But, I kept at it obsessively and, sure enough, my back pain returned, not so much from my muscle-tearing swings that thudded into the ground, but surely from the bending necessary to repair my deep divots. When I left the many pockmarked public courses I played on, I avoided contact with people who might have seen me play.

I finally broke 120, but I understood by that time that golf is really hard for seniors. It's a great game for the roughly ten percent of us who are "naturals" and for those of us who learned the game when we were young, but not for your average Joe. To me, the really good players are geniuses, like Einstein or Picasso. You just don't learn how to become a genius, you are or you aren't. If you're not, you suffer, or, if you're smart and healthy in the head, you accept it. But, being who I am, there was no way I could.

With time, however, I became cautiously optimistic that I would break 110, even though, deep down, I understood that the golf course was really a field of dreams and a nightmare for most players.

All golfers imagine playing that one great game one great day, driving the ball a mile, sinking the long putt and basking in the envy our friends. My scores actually did improve. I began to shoot 115, then sometimes even 110, and I knew, just knew, that I would soon break 100, the duffer's Holy Grail. But, it never happened! I never broke 100. It's been years and I'm still shooting between 103 and 108. Besides, my back hurts like hell.

My wife left me just about the time that I was improving because, she cried, the marriage didn't exist since I was never home. She said that I spent all my time playing or purchasing all sorts of crap in the nearby golf shop. She never saw me on weekends, as I was always too exhausted after playing to leave my bed.

My friends shunned me because I played too slowly. Even the beginners didn't play with me. Last month, my doctor told me the aches and pains in my joints were not from ordinary arthritis, but from Lyme's disease, because of some frigging tick bite I got searching for lost balls in the rough.

In addition to all these problems, I was hemorrhaging money. So I got the stupid idea of betting my buddies on the games. After all, I had this huge handicap. Unfortunately, I lost five dollars here, a tener there and even more on moronic side bets. At first, the money didn't seem like much. But, when you play several times a week and add up the cost of greens fees, lessons, new clubs and an occasional fancy golf bag, your head starts to spin. And what about the additional expense of subscribing to The Golf Channel and golf magazine? I barely covered the costs with my measly paycheck from my work. Last week, I started to compare prices for bars of soap at Wal-Mart's.

What aggravated me the most was that perfect strangers, such as that aged and wrinkled Guatemalan associate groundskeeper, were asking me to play. I decided to stop betting on games, but then I had a hard time finding guys to play with.

I was flummoxed, but, luckily, within a few days, a solution popped into my head after reading about a lawsuit brought by some schlimazel who was hit on his head by an errant golf ball while walking innocently on a street just outside the course. The plaintiff was awarded a bundle for "pain and suffering." I reasoned that with my back problem and angst with my game, I too was having "pain and suffering." It made sense to me that I should be remunerated. I reasoned that my aggravation with golf and my loss of big bucks could be assuaged somewhat, if the golf club paid me if I had a lousy day! Why not?

Let's assume I had a good day, shot 98, played in only 3 1/2 hours, and didn't lose any balls. If that occurred, why not pay the bastards their usual fee! But, if I played miserably, lost dozens of balls and wasted an irritating 6 hours on the course, $50 would be a reasonable amount *for me* to receive from the Pro Shop till. And, for a real aggravating, 6-hour round, with a score of, say, 114, I wanted to get paid something more. $100 would do the trick. If, in addition, I had to see my chiropractor or my Lyme's disease specialist, I wanted bigger bucks, maybe $120. After all, that only amounts to $20 an hour, just a little more than the Guatemalan gets who cuts the fairway grass. The whole idea seemed reasonable to me.

I'm still searching for some sport that I can enjoy and maybe excel at. By chance, last week, after watching badminton on ESPN, I surfed the channels and saw Tiger playing. It all seemed so easy, so natural. For a brief moment, I wondered. Maybe? Just maybe...No! Schmuck. You know what will happen.

That morning, I decided to revisit the pro shop in order to peddle my golf clubs, bag, and a load of scuffed nameless golf balls, but I had no luck. Dispirited, I exited the clubhouse and headed for the parking lot. On the way, I passed the first hole. There were some old timers teeing off and I could swear I heard one of them exclaim, "O.K. guys, let's get it over with!" Smart guy, I thought to myself.

The Meeting

Max Bernstein and Stuart Cohen had been meeting for over ten years at Harry's bar in Chelsea. They met at the popular watering hole every Thursday at about five, talking and laughing while downing a few bottles of beer. They had been close friends for over 50 years. Stu became a dermatologist while Max took over his father's successful brassier business, *Bernstein's Bras*. The meetings were only interrupted during the summer when they both vacationed.

The bar seemed busier than usual. The rhythmic thudding of loud rap music permeated the crowded space. Stu wondered if meeting at Harry's wasn't a bad idea; perhaps a quieter place would have been preferable.

"So, what's new, Max?" Stu had noticed that Max was a little perkier than usual.

"Have I got something to tell you, Stu!" He leaned closer and stared at Stu like a dog at its master.

"I bumped into Charlie yesterday."

" Charlie? Charlie Stone? You got to be kidding? "

Charlie, Stu, and Max had been classmates in high school in Brooklyn during the early forties. Oddly enough, they were all children of Depression-traumatized parents, but Stu and Max came from middle-class families. Charlie's father died when he was a kid and his mother supported him by working as a waitress at a local greasy spoon. They all played on the high-school basketball team. The handsome Charlie made All-City in their senior year and was, by far, the most gifted athlete of them all, as well as being the most popular kid at school. Stu and Max drifted away from him for no particular reason, but they kept up with each other's lives through conversations with classmates and friends from Brooklyn.

"So what did he say, Max?"

"He said he'd love to see ya."

"I'd really like to see him, too."

"Stu, I didn't recognize him at first. He came over to greet me at a party. He looked vaguely familiar, but I couldn't place him. He just looked like a bald old man." Max still had curly, blond hair, protruding ears, and a wire-thin body. When they met, Charlie had a well-groomed, red beard and mustache. But the striking thing about him was that he was so huge that the baggy, navy-blue suit he wore seemed to droop and be fashioned by gravity."

"Stu, he gave me his number. He said he wondered what the Hell happened to you."

Max gave Stu the number and they reminisced about Charlie for the next hour or so. They each ordered their last beer, and at about six thirty, they parted. Max drove home to Riverdale and Stu drove to his apartment on Fifth Avenue.

As Stu entered his apartment, he realized that Fern was on the telephone.

"I'm on the phone with Gladys," she yelled from their den. "I'll be off in a minute." Although Fern just loved talking on the phone, Stu disliked it and hated answering it even more. He also disliked small talk, and wondered if these aversions were related to his busy dermatological practice where he was constantly on the phone and talking to and caring for scores of patients, many of who were new. Psychiatrists must be the same way, he reasoned. The thought of psychiatrists made him think of Max, who had been seeing one for decades, about "marital problems."

Even though he hadn't thought about Charlie for many years, now that his name surfaced, Stu realized how close the two of them had once been, how crazy they both were for the Knicks and how much they had enjoyed being with each other. He wondered why he hadn't contacted Charlie just to say hello, maybe to arrange to have a drink or two.

He thought inertia, maybe just plain laziness, was probably the reason most of the time.

Fern walked into the family room where Stu was now reading *The New York Times*. She gave him a perfunctory kiss and sat down next to him. He couldn't wait to tell her about someone they both knew in high school.

"Who? What are you talking about?" Fern asked.

"Charlie Stone."

"Charlie Stone?"

"Yup. Max told me he met him last week at a party on the Upper West Side." Max was there with Harriet, his sensational-looking wife who had flaming red hair and soft facial features. Unfortunately she was not too smart, a *little light in the head* as Max used to say when confiding to Stu.

Fern and Harriet had little in common, so Fern preferred not to see her socially. Stu wasn't happy about her feelings. She suggested that he arrange to see Max alone, without her, probably best on Thursday nights, when she played indoor tennis.

"Max gave me his number, and I'm going to call him. I'm busy all next week with meetings and patients, but I've got Wednesday evening free. I'll see if that's OK with him. Fern, I hope you don't mind me doing it Wednesday?" Fern had no objection.

He called Charlie on Friday. Sally, his wife, answered the phone and they spoke briefly. When Charlie got on the phone, Stu felt a little anxious. Charlie told him how happy he was that he called and how surprised he was to see Max, but admitted that Max looked much older than he expected.

Charlie agreed that dinner next Wednesday would be fine and he immediately suggested that they dine at a midtown restaurant near where he worked. He told Stu that he'd wear a red carnation in his jacket lapel. Stu laughed, not quite sure if he was kidding.

After office hours on Wednesday, Stu drove downtown and was lucky to find a garage next door to the restaurant. After pulling in, an attendant gave him a ticket and he handed him the keys. He also noticed another very obese attendant who happened to have a small black mole on the left side of his forehead. He was constantly looking at moles in the office and unconsciously continued to do so when he was just walking in the city, going to parties or talking to friends or relatives. As he left the garage, he no longer thought about it and headed to the nearby restaurant.

Charlie had not yet arrived, so Stu sat at the bar and watched news on TV. In the middle of a segment on Iraq, he felt a tap on his shoulder. It was obviously Charlie, an obese Charlie, but still good-looking, with a huge red carnation in his lapel. They embraced and patted each other's shoulders. Stu immediately saw a large mole on the left side of his forehead, almost identical in location and shape to the one he saw on the attendant in the garage. Charlie worked as a garage attendant? He tried to appear unperturbed, but heard little of what Charlie said for the next few moments.

"Didn't you hear me, Stu, I said how the Hell are you?"

"G-great. Just great, Charlie. And you?"

"Fine. Just fine."

"So, what ya been up to, old buddy?" Stu asked. "The last time I saw you--God it must have been decades ago-- weren't you the manager at Modell's, that sporting goods store on 42nd Street, and I was just starting medical school?"

"Yeah. I left there after a year and then worked as a bartender at The Three Musketeer's in the Bronx. It folded a year after I started there. I liked the work, but Sally always complained about the hours. After that, I was unemployed for..."

Stu interrupted him. He couldn't bear to hear the rest of his story.

"How did you end up parking cars?"

"How did you know I worked in a parking lot?" Charlie asked.

"I had just parked there this afternoon, and as I was leaving, I saw an attendant with a blackish mole on his forehead. If that was you, you were bringing a car to someone, a Lincoln Town car, I think."

"You're right about the car. It was a Lincoln. Mr. Shapiro owns it. He's a great tipper. Three bucks at a clip." Stu cringed.

"But, how'd you end up working there?

"Well, after the restaurant, I took odd jobs. I worked at a hardware store in Riverdale but I got fired because I came in a little late now and then. I then drove a cab for a year. Sally was always bugging me to take a job working for her first cousin, Sam, in his mid-town garage. He offered me the job at a family wedding right after I left driving cabs. I really didn't like Sam, but, honestly, I needed the money. He was always bragging about the celebrities who parked their cars in his lot and how well he did in the market. You know the type. Who gives a shit about his celebrities and how much money he has or they have? But, Sally prevailed, and about three years ago, I took the job. I wasn't happy about it, although Sam said that if things worked out, I would switch from parking cars to some type of managerial position. What can you say? You gotta do what you gotta do. Now, even though I don't make much money, I'm glad I got the job because I speak to a lot of guys nowadays who can't find work. It came just at the right time because I was starting to lose confidence in myself. I felt I was a loser.

"Wow. I never imagined that you'd think that way, Charlie. Never. I always figured you were so self-confident that you felt like you'd succeed in anything you did."

"I only wish."

Stu wondered if Charlie was maybe *flawed* in some way or if he just had bad breaks, as he got older. No matter, he admired his pluck.

They were both starved, so Charlie hailed the waiter who took them to their table.

Stu was unhappy when Charlie finally asked him about *his* work. He couldn't bear to describe the success he'd had in the last few years. He'd lie, he thought. Then he realized that was ridiculous, and he told him about his practice, emphasizing the problems with HMO's, deadbeats and malpractice. He mentioned his two kids, Philip and Jill, who were both happily married with kids of their own.

He then inquired about Charlie's children. As soon as he asked, he regretted it.

"We have no kids. Sally lost twins when she was four months pregnant about thirty years ago."

He berated himself for asking and changed the subject by asking Charlie about the mole on his forehead. Charlie felt funny discussing it with him. Stu was sure it was benign, but wondered if it bothered Charlie cosmetically, because if it did, he felt it could be removed and leave only a small scar. Charlie just shrugged his shoulders. Stu was used to being asked about moles at parties and elsewhere, but this was the first time he brought the subject up himself.

"Thanks for asking, Stu."

It was an emotional evening and Stu was relieved when it was over. He offered to give Charlie a ride home, but he said that he had some things to do in mid-town. They shook hand, embraced briefly and agreed to meet again.

Stu replayed the entire evening's conversation in his mind during his ride home. He was anxious to discuss the meeting with Fern, but could absolutely not wait until his meeting the next night with Max.

"So? So what happened?" Fern asked as soon as he entered the apartment.

They sat on a couch and Fern listened carefully to what Stu had to say. She couldn't believe what he said, but told him that she heard years ago that Charlie had a drinking problem. Maybe that was the reason he couldn't hold a job. They spoke about a friend who recently become an alcoholic and argued about its cause. They went to bed early.

Thursday was a busy day in the office, but Stu was preoccupied with thinking about meeting Max. Over the years, he had learned to dismiss any distracting thoughts when caring for patients. His staff was warned not to buzz him if he was in a room with a patient; he'd prefer to call back later when he was between rooms or after hours. When he himself visited doctors, he resented them taking calls. It was sometimes even apparent that the calls were from friends or relatives who just wanted to chat.

Max was sitting at the bar, nursing his beer and staring into space.

"Hey, Max. How ya doing?" Max straightened up.

"Things are not good Stu. I got problems."

"What? What's the matter? Sounds like you *do* have problems."

"Harriet and I are getting divorced. It just isn't working out. We're just wrong for each other. I guess I knew it from the beginning, but refused to accept it." He bit his lips and narrowed his eyes.

Stu studied his face. He started to feel that same empathy he felt for Charlie. He felt drained, weakened, like from fever. His otherwise placid, unruffled world was turning upside down and he felt vulnerable.

The Perils Of Cocktail Parties

Last summer, Claire and I received an invitation to a cocktail party. The white card was rimmed with small gold stars and, in the center, were ever-enlarging green bubbles floating out of purple cocktail glasses. Within the graphics were the time, date and location and the usual RSVP. I didn't want to waste a Saturday night in August awash in small talk. Almost everyone invited surely was going to be from the country club and conversation would eventually revolve around tennis and tennis shots and golf and golf shots, but also, golf swings. My tennis was so-so, but my golf scores, golf shots, and golf swings were all pathetic.

I showed the invitation to a nearly hoarse Claire just as she had completed her ritual morning-marathon phone calls to Carol and Sylvia.

"The Winigers are having a cocktail party. But, I'm telling you right now. *I'm not going!*" I declared.

Claire studied the card, brushing her long silvery hair away from her pretty face. She ignored my decision. It was as if she didn't hear me. She opened her appointment book, flipped through a few pages, and pointed to an unmarked Saturday, August eighth. She grabbed a ball-point pen and wrote next to the date: *Winiger-6:30.*

"Claire, I'm not going! You know how I hate cocktail parties. And besides Bill Winiger is a bore, nice guy, but a bore. I bumped into him at the club the other day and realized he has absolutely nothing to say. All he can talk about is his fucking button business. No, I'm absolutely not going. I'm starting to think that maybe I just don't belong at our golf club. You do! I don't!"

125

Claire had heard this story before. It surfaced every time they were invited somewhere. I *did* enjoy dining out with one or two couples, but hated going to large parties, especially weddings, bar mitzvahs or cocktail parties. I believed that the larger the social group, the less interested the people were in what *you* had to say, and the more they would slyly search for other higher-profile party goers. It was mob psychology and everyone in the mob knew the rules.

I was adamant even though Claire knew from experience that I was a pussycat, but this time, she started to sulk and it bothered me. I wanted to be left alone for a few moments and think this thing through, so I told Claire that I had to go to the John.

What bothered me most was that, because I was a dermatologist, cheapskates would often approach me at cocktail parties and ask me just to take a "look" at a mole on their face or arms and I usually didn't have the guts to say no. Although I had 20/20 vision, lately, in order to frustrate such aggravating encounters, I began to carry thick coke-bottle spectacles in my jacket pocket and would whip them out when queried about something dermatological. I sometimes made my head and hands totter a tad to further exaggerate the ruse. I then would say to the freeloader, "Make an appointment and see me in my office where I have better lighting." Invariably, they never showed up. I wondered if it wouldn't be better to tell guests at these parties that I was a gynecologist. Better still, a proctologist.

Early in my practice, a very close medical colleague, Eli Rabinowitz, asked me about an itchy rash in his groin. Eli and I interned together so I suggested looking at it in a nearby bathroom. With Eli's thighs spread wide, his jewels elevated with his right hand, crumpled trousers lowered just over his Docksiders, I stooped low and close and peered into his groin. Just at that moment, Herman Berman, a yenta if there ever was one, came by, quickly glanced at us, excused himself and disappeared with gossip written all over his ugly face.

I decided not to aggravate Claire since I knew she had complained the night before about the return of her chronic sciatic pain and she felt shitty because an aunt who she adored who had just been told that she had breast cancer.

"Harry, this whole thing is ridiculous, absolutely ridiculous. What's going on with you? This stubbornness about cocktail parties has got to stop. What am I supposed to do when you sit home and watch your stupid TV programs rather than go out."

I wanted to give in. It really wasn't the end of the world, but I couldn't help responding to her. "You call Public Television, C-Span II and The History Channel stupid? Come on Claire, let's be reasonable. I never said I didn't want to go out at all, did I? I just hate going to those crowded cocktail parties. *You invited me to your cocktail party so I'm obliged to invite you to mine--* even though we rarely socialize. Ugh!

"Claire, you know I'd much prefer to dine out with just one or two other couples, friends who we've known a long time and like. Even then, despite our good intentions, you know what often happens. The Rabinowitz's ask if we can be joined by the O'Briens and the O'Briens ask if the Cohens can join us, and in no time, the date mushrooms into double or triple the original number. Worse, I invariably end up in a corner seat at a long rectangular table far removed from the people I originally intended to dine with."

I headed to the living room, really pissed, probably more so with myself than with Claire. I plopped into my womb chair and picked up the TV remote and turned on the TV.

Claire followed me and spoke in a conciliatory, but firm tone, overcoming the noise of the TV whose volume I had purposefully raised. "Fine! We won't go to the cocktail party. I was never wild about Kate Wilinger anyway. It's just that I've known her since high school. But, I guess people do change, and we really have grown apart. And, you're right, Bill is a bore. I'm so accustomed to automatically saying yes to an invitation. Let's ask the Epsteins if they want to join us for dinner instead, just the four of us. We haven't seen Adele and Abe in a while. Funny, I spoke to her a few weeks ago and she wondered why we haven't seen each other in a long time. By the way, she started taking art classes at the Y. She's swooning over her teacher, a real hunk, she said. Isn't that funny? You remember that I spoke about the classes last month. I'd love to speak to her about it.

"Fine with me, Claire, I'd love to see them. It's such a coincidence, but I saw Abe in the office last month, and I wondered why we haven't seen him and Adele in a while." I started to wrap my arms around Clair's waist, but she had already scurried off to call Adele.

"Claire make the dinner reservations for four at Le Mistral and please, please, just don't tell anyone."

The Telephone Call

Hudsonville is a mid-sized town nestled among a profusion of tall evergreens that overlooks the eastern shore of the Hudson River. It's about forty-five miles north of New York City. The community has been around for about a century and a half and is little different than other river towns with its slow pace, unremarkable, red-brick, one-to-two-story commercial buildings, and people who all seem to know one another and take pride in their quaint historic town with breath taking river views from many of their homes.

Harry Fretting and his wife Delores lived there in a home on West Elm but lacked those views. Their house was close to Main Street where Harry worked, together with Gus Thompson and Frank Santucci, at Hudson Shoes. Sam Mizer was their boss.

Outwardly, one would think that life was not bad for the Frettings, especially since their son Matt just got into Yale and was about to marry a local girl the Frettings adore. Laura, their daughter, married a few years ago and had two children.

Harry usually had an easy walk to work, but, today, in mid-February, heavy snow blanketed the street and a brisk wind was blowing from the northeast. Fortunately, he was dressed warmly. A wooly gray hat, the type worn by Russians, framed his large head. In the center of his chubby face was a bulbous nose, reddened by a bad cold, the freezing weather, and his fondness for cheap, red wine. A minute, cone-shaped drop of water dangled precariously from the undersurface of his nose. He seemed to be struggling down Main Street, being weighed down by his

225-pound body, compressed into little over five feet. He was wary of his movements and attempts to dodge icy patches and slush that coated the sidewalk. Harry's old, high rubber boots constricted the bottom of his pants. Everybody knows that he is no dresser. This morning he was wearing Hunter's green slacks and a beat-out old borsht-colored shirt with white dots throughout. Here and there, the shirt was tarnished with assorted spots of past meals. He was blanketed in a black greatcoat.

It took Harry more time today to get to work than usual. After 27 years, he was Mr. Mizer's most trusted employee and the first who arrived every morning.

The weather was not the only thing on Harry's mind. Money was. Delores lost her job as a secretary at the high school last week, and although her salary was not great, it did matter. His stock-market investments, intended to provide for Matt's education, had soured and last month's trip to Hawaii cost more than he intended to spend. Yes, Harry definitely needed a raise. He hadn't had one in four years.

Mizer arrived seconds after Harry. "Good morning, Sam," Harry yelled, before he unlocked the front door, stomping his feet to dislodge snow from his boots.

"It's really not such a good morning, Harry. I almost slipped in front of Cookie's Bakery. Wouldn't be such a bad deal though if I fell," Mizer said with a smiling face. "Old man Cookie is loaded, and uncleared ice could cost him a bundle in court."

Hudsonville Shoes had chartreuse-colored, wall-to wall, slightly frayed carpeting on the floor; it was definitely not Karastan. Scattered haphazardly were several elongated low stools with seats covered in cracked red-leather on which the salesmen sat to do their fittings. A purplish curtain acted as a door and led into a large, shoebox-filled, storage room. The place looked garish and dingy. It was decorated like Harry was dressed.

The 68-year-old Mizer was over six-feet tall, thin, almost gaunt. His face was distinctly oval and his red hair was bushy on the sides but absent on the crown. A sizeable aquiline nose and a drooping handlebar mustache accentuated the elongation of his face. Unlike Harry, he was dressed conservatively in dark colors. His low-keyed dress was in keeping with his conservative financial outlook, but clashed dramatically with his yen for ribbing and telling smutty jokes to anyone within earshot. Mizer always seemed in good spirits, except for the rare occasions when he surreptitiously placed small, white tablets under his tongue. Harry liked Sam and enjoyed being around him, although he could do without the jokes. Gus and Frank, however, loved the stories.

The opening of the front door interrupted Harry' musing. The first customer of the day was entering and *shoes, shoes, and more shoes* soon become the only thing on Harry's mind, until noon at least, when he will eat and schmooze across the street at Willie's Luncheonette.

Harry did fairly well in the morning, sold several pairs of shoes and a couple of pairs of socks. Before noon, he was a little tired, probably from his cold. He decided he'd have a cup of tea with his lunch instead of his usual soda.

The luncheonette was busy. His sat down at a table with a friend from bowling. His ham-and-Swiss on rye (with a generous schmear of Guldens) tasted great. He ended up having two cups of tea. As usual, he left Pearl, the waitress, a generous tip.

As Harry crossed the street to go back to the store, he noted that patches of snow were dappled with sparkling, yellow light as the sun struggled to shine through the mass of grayish clouds. Fretting was buoyed by the promising weather and expectations of an afternoon filled with potential customers. After all, most of his pay depended on commissions from the sale of shoes, especially if he sold two to the same customer, although he also got additional money from sales of socks, shoe polish, laces and other accessories.

The last customers of the day, a chubby teenage boy and his slim, blond-haired mother, were looking for a pair of shoes for the boy's upcoming birthday party. The mother liked a pair of dark-chocolate-colored Oxfords that she saw in the window. They were marked $49.99 and had been advertised at that price in the ad that Mizer took out in the Hudsonville Bee. For some reason, Harry was sure that they were $59.99. After hearing Harry's price, the mother knitted her eyebrows quizzically, and in a voice slightly louder than Harry's, pointed to the window and said "But the price of the shoes is clearly marked $49.99. Go look at it yourself." As Harry went to the window, he immediately realized he made a mistake because Sam had told him the previous week that the shoes were being discontinued and the price reduced. The shoes fit the boy just fine and Harry apologized for the mix-up. Sam was in earshot of the conversation, but gave no indication that he overheard them. Harry thought to himself that today was not the time to screw up. He realized that he had been so preoccupied with the raise that he forgot things and was not being as alert as he usually was.

Within minutes before closing, the store was empty, and the skies were darkening again, foreboding more bad weather. Harry doubted any more customers would appear. "Time to talk turkey!" he thought.

Mizer was busy in the storage room when Harry entered. "Sam, could I talk to you about something for a moment?"

"Why sure, Harry, come on back here." Sam responded in a friendly manner.

As Harry pushed aside the curtain to enter the room, the slight cough and sniffles that he had all day seemed to worsen. Mizer was seated at a small, white plastic table, in the corner, near the back window, barely visible because of the 40-Watt light bulbs he used to illuminate the storage room.

"How can I help you Harry?" Mizer asked.

"Sam, I've been working for you for..." He started, but was interrupted by the ringing of the telephone on Mizer's desk. Mizer picked up the telephone and spoke to the caller. He excused himself, signaling to Harry that he wanted some privacy by raising his left hand and flapping it gently back and forth. Harry got the message and retreated to the back of the dusty room, awkwardly trying to appear preoccupied by arranging a few stray shoeboxes onto their proper shelves.

"Yes?" Mizer said to the caller. " Oh, Johnny, it's you. Thanks for calling, but you got me at a bad time. I've got to talk to Harry. Can I call you back? Where are you? Fine. I'll call back shortly."

Harry wondered what Sam would be talking to Johnny about. Sam had recently joked to Harry about retiring to Florida and selling the store and Johnny was Mizer's accountant, as well as being his best friend. After Sam hung up the phone, Harry returned to him. Just then, he felt a tickle inside his nose, and before he could retrieve his handkerchief from his back pants-pocket, he sneezed. The sneeze was powerful, a sneeze unlike any he had ever sneezed before. The watery explosion splattered over Sam's desk, moistening some checks he was signing. The deluge had even reached the old man's favorite snack, a small Hostess Cherry Pie, which was lying half opened on the desk.

Oh, my God! Harry thought. What the hell did I do?

Almost simultaneous with the sneeze, Sam bolted upright from his chair, tilted backward, almost falling over in his excitement. Harry wanted to wipe some of the droplets (one was flecked with yellow) from Mizer's shirt, but he immediately realized he would compound the problem by using his soiled hanky.

Jesus, of all the times to fuck up, Harry thought to himself. He looked at Mizer, who was wiping off both his shirt and the mess on the desk, when he realized his boss had a faint smile on his face. No, Harry realized, Sam was not angry, or even annoyed. In fact, the old guy was starting to smile.

"Goddam, Harry. That was a whopper of a sneeze, man. You could have parted the Red Sea with that one." Almost immediately, Sam was laughing so loud that Harry started to smile sheepishly. He was relieved but at the same time wanted to disappear.

"So, Harry, what did you want to talk to me about?" asked his boss.

Harry saw that Sam was back to his old self. Maybe the sneeze was a propitious omen. This was definitely a good time to ask for the raise. They discussed the matter for a few minutes in a business-like manner. Harry wasn't sure if Mizer understood how important the raise was. He didn't tell him that Delores's job, as a teacher's assistant, was lost because of budget cuts. He felt it just wouldn't be right.

Harry was making roughly $30,000 to $35,000 dollars a year depending on his commissions and asked for a $5, 000 raise, but was probably willing to take $ 4,000.

"Harry, you know if I give you a raise, Gus and Frank will surely find out. They'll also want a raise. With the economy as lousy as it is now, I don't think the store could handle it. You know...let me think about it. I'll call you over the weekend." Harry wasn't sure what Sam would do, but he did know that Mizer lived well. He had no children.

As Harry surveyed the scene of the accident, a casual glance at the moistened half-eaten cherry pie reminded him that when he was in the luncheonette a few weeks ago, he overheard someone say that Sam's real name was Mintzer, but everybody felt it more appropriate to call him Mizer.

As Harry was leaving, Sam said, "Harry, with your cold, maybe you should leave earlier today. I'll stay late and close up. It'll be a good time to go over some paperwork that's been accumulating."

"Fine," agreed Harry.

"I'll call you over the weekend. Will you be home?" Sam inquired.

"No problem. I'll be around the house all weekend. There's some good football being played. Call me anytime."

It was dark outside when Harry left and began his trudge up the hill. Traffic on Main Street was starting to pick up. Yellow headlights were everywhere. People were arriving from work in New York and going home. Despite the busy and upbeat atmosphere, Harry was feeling dispirited. Delores greeted him with a kiss and offered him some red jug wine from Gallo. He began to mellow. They laughed when he told her about the day's *accident.* Harry correctly thought Sam wouldn't call that night, expecting the call Saturday or Sunday.

Saturday was usually devoted to household chores. He fixed a toaster handle that had just broken last week and repaired a kitchen chair, one of whose legs had cracked. He thought that he really should lose some weight, since it was his chair, not Delores,' that broke. The telephone rang once late in the afternoon. It was Delores' sister calling to chat. Before Harry knew it, it was close to 11. He started to read the local paper, but soon dozed off in his easy chair. Delores nudged him gently and suggested he go to bed. He got up, staggered to the bedroom and fell asleep again.

He awoke early on Sunday morning and while eating bacon and eggs thought of Mizer who never ate bacon or pork. He was a pious man who had a liberal and leftist outlook on life. That boded well for Harry to get the raise. Surely, his boss would call today.

Delores returned home late on Sunday afternoon after visiting a neighbor. Harry soon realized that the weekend was almost over and Sam had yet to call. It was not like him.

On his way to the john, Harry passed a wall phone and was struck by the fact that the phone had suddenly taken on an importance far beyond what it should. After all, it was just a lowly combination of mundane materials like plastics, metals and wires. Although the individual ingredients probably cost peanuts, when combined, they became capable of changing one's life. He likened it to some type of idol with scary imagined power. It could bring good news or bad, or even fatal news, and as he realized all day Sunday, no news, almost the worst of all the possible outcomes. He thought about all those times he waited anxiously by the phone for a doctor's call to give him the results of some X ray or blood test. He almost began to resent the phone's power, but the thought seemed ridiculous to him. This whole thing was starting to make him nuts. He thought very briefly about calling Sam, but after discussing it with Delores, decided it would not be a good idea.

That evening, Harry had a dream. The phone had rung and he barely heard it because he had become unexplainably deaf. He picked the phone up and realized it was Mizer but was unable to hear what he was saying, even though Sam began to talk louder and louder, eventually actually screaming. Harry became agitated, then, terrified, and thought he was going to die. He awoke trembling, but slowly calmed down when he realized it was only a dream. He had no idea of the time; it was still dark outside. He looked at the white plastic Westclox on his night table and was surprised that the green luminescent hands indicated that it was already 7:14 in the morning. His activity awoke Delores and he told her of his dream. She didn't even try to interpret it; rather, she tenderly put her hands around his neck, looked him straight in the eyes, and in a whisper, suggested that they should consider a vacation after this whole nightmare was over. She thought a cruise, perhaps to the Caribbean, might be ideal. Touched, Harry kissed her gently and simply said, "Delores, I love you."

Surprisingly, he had lost his appetite for breakfast, barely drinking his cup of coffee. He wanted to get to work. Harry was starting to get a little annoyed with Sam. After he rose from the kitchen table, he impulsively dashed to the wall phone and picked it up just to be sure there was a dial tone and that it was working. The dial tone was just fine. Delores wondered what was really going on, but by the time she decided to question Harry, he had already dressed and left the house.

Because the weather had improved, he arrived at the store in no time, and did some work in the storeroom. He returned to the front of the store just as Frank arrived, but Sam had yet to arrive. Gus generally came in a little later than everybody else because he had to tend to an invalid sister who lived with him. Harry was headed toward the plastic racks at the front of the store to rearrange some of the socks, when the phone rang. To Frank's surprise, Harry rushed to answer the phone first, even though Frank was closer. In Harry's rush, he almost knocked over one of the fitting stools.

"Hello?" he blurted.

"Harry? Is this Harry?" said the voice on the other end. The voice sounded familiar, but Harry couldn't place it.

"Yes," Harry said. "Who is this?"

"Harry, it's Johnny. Johnny Belsito. You know, Sam's good friend. Remember, I was in the store several months ago to talk to Sam. He introduced us. Remember?"

"Yeah", Harry said. "I remember. How ya' doing? How can I help you? Sam's not in yet." Harry thought he heard a faint sob on the phone. The line almost seemed like it had gone dead for a moment or two. "Hello? Hello? Johnny, are you still there?" he asked.

"Yeah. Harry...Harry... I have bad news. Terrible news," Johnny said in a deep, solemn voice.

"What? What? What's happened?" Harry asked, but was afraid of the answer.

Johnny had broken down now and was on the verge of crying. "Sam died last night," Johnny said. "He had a heart attack. I knew he had heart trouble, but, with Sam, it was always something to joke about. Who knew how sick he was," Johnny said.

"Oh, how terrible. It's hard to believe. How's Molly taking it? Mizer told me that she lost her only brother a year ago. How's she doing?"

"She's a mess. I just got to their house," Johnny said.

"Can I talk to her?" asked Harry.

"No." Johnny responded. "She's not up to talking to anyone right now. The funeral's Wednesday noon at Lamberts."

The death of Sam rattled Harry. He remembered how he had spent more time with Sam than anyone else in this whole world other than Delores--more time than with his brother who lived nearby. Six days a week, Harry and Sam shared their thoughts, nothing deep and philosophical, but mundane, ordinary thoughts. Of course, shoes were the major topic, but Harry liked Mizer's overall values, except when it came to money.

The funeral was what one would expect. Everybody moved in slow motion and looked worried. Mourners spoke in hushed voices, although a few, probably long-lost relatives, spoke animatedly to each other as if at a cocktail party. A ghostly-looking Molly looked lost and more fragile than Harry remembered her to be. Sam's sister led her to her seat, supporting her flail arms with her hands. Everybody pondered their own death, who and how many of their friends would attend their funeral and, of course, what would be said.

Harry and Delores sat several rows behind Frank and his wife. The rabbi spoke about someone he really knew and liked, not someone he was briefed about a day before the services by grieving family members. Sam was active in the temple, giving much of his time to charitable causes.

Harry sniffled and narrowed his eyes, trying to avoid crying, at the rabbi's mention of Sam's easy ways with people. At the conclusion of the service, Harry noted Johnny exiting as he and Delores were filing out. Harry whispered "Johnny!" Johnny turned and greeted Harry warmly with his raised right hand. "Hi. Hi, Harry."

The mourners were gathered outside the temple, some preparing to go home and resume their lives, probably a little guiltily, or to work or to attend the internment. The immediate family was heading to a black stretch limousine parked at the side of the temple. They would mourn further at the burial site. From the corner of Harry's eye, he saw Johnny emerging from the exiting crowd and approaching him.

"Harry, I'd like to speak to you about something. It's rather important. Give me your home telephone number. Do you have a pencil and paper?" asked Belsito. Harry began to feel in his pockets, but realized he didn't.

"Johnny. No, I don't. You know what. My number is easy to remember. 591-592-5259. I'm on Elm, 22 Elm, in case you forget the number."

"I'll call you in a few days, maybe over the weekend," Belsito said. "It's about you and the store." His voice trailed off as they separated.

Me and the store? What the hell does that mean? Harry wondered about the possibility that they might close the store and he'd be out of a job. On the ride home, he asked

Delores what she thought of the remark. She admitted she had no idea, but deep down, she thought of him being without a job and that frightened her.

Sergio And Anna

Sergio was still sleeping when Anna was awoken by the high-pitched sound of bells warning that railroad gates were closing. The road leading across the tracks was barely visible in the bluish morning fog. Rain had fallen during the night. As the train hurtled southward, clusters of whitewashed houses, some with lights on and some with ribbons of grayish smoke ambling skyward, began to dot the rural landscape, announcing the arrival of dawn. Anna wondered if she too wasn't beginning a new life, but with someone who was ready to explode, almost like a suicide bomber, who would take her with him. Sergio worried her. Just as dark and ominous thoughts flooded her mind, she sensed that he was awakening

"Jesus Christ. Are you OK?" he muttered, as he turned toward her window seat.

"Why? What's the matter?" Anna whispered.

"I had this frightening dream about you. Thank God, it really was a dream, but, ... he muttered, his voice trailing off as he stared into space.

"Do you want to talk about it?" she inquired.

"No!"

"OK OK"

"Are you hungry, Sergio? It's about six. I think we have some bread and grapes left over." She looked under her seat for the brown, crumpled bag with the food.

"Yeah. Grapes would be just fine."

He took the bag from her and looked inside, but turned away when he saw that the green-colored grapes had a few flecks of brown scattered over the skin. Anna could sense that he was getting annoyed. She was used to his irritability. He reminded her of her father, even in his looks. Sergio was in his early 50's, his brownish hair graying at the temples and his prominent chin squared. He looked sexy in the dark interior of the train.

"We should arrive in about half an hour," Anna said.

Sergio scanned the interior of the train, looked at the ceiling lights, then at the floor and pointed to the their seats. "God aren't they awful, not only ugly looking but so uncomfortable!" Anna looked at the faded burgundy-colored fabric that covered their seats. To her, the color was kind of cool and the seats themselves were just fine." Was there anything they agreed upon, she wondered?

The morning mist had completely dissipated now and rural Spain was coming into focus. A young man in a frayed beret was walking alone on a hardscrabble road in the mid-distance. A large wooden cart, with a broken wheel, was strewn on the road and partially blocked the stroller's way. Everyone's got problems, she mused, as the scene hurried by.

"Gee, I'm sort of nauseous. I don't feel well," Anne said. "Wonder what I could have eaten? Probably that chicken salad last night. She remembered leaving most of it over because of a sour taste. Most of the meals they had in Barcelona were great because Sergio knew local reporters there who suggested restaurants when they first arrived about two months ago. He was writing an article on Gaudi for a struggling, monthly art magazine in Madrid. Anna was an up-and-coming sculptor who had just had a successful show in a prominent gallery in downtown Madrid just before she met Sergio at the party.

Even with rouge on, Anna's cheeks barely looked healthy. She was not pretty, but she was aristocratic looking with an upturned nose, blue eyes and hair in a pageboy. She was neatly dressed in a black skirt and colorful blouse.

Sergio was standing now, yawning as he narrowed his eyes and hunched his shoulders in an attempt to peer out of the fogged window. "The nausea is probably from the kid," he whispered nonchalantly.

Anna's thoughts roamed backward to three months ago when they both became stinking drunk at Antonio and Isabella's blast in Madrid. She was sure it was the week before she got pregnant. It was definitely not what she had planned or wished. She loved her freedom to work and study. Sergio was all over her from the moment she arrived and although there was something vaguely attractive about him, she was wary, but not wary enough to resist dating him from then on.

Suddenly, Anna realized that Sergio was asking her something, but she had been too preoccupied with thoughts of that night to hear him.

"Anna! Anna! Did you hear anything I've just said? Anything? Where the Hell have you been for the last few minutes?" Sergio was now sitting next to her. He paused, wrinkling his brow and scrutinizing her. He thrust his face toward her.

"Oh. I'm sorry," Anna said. "I was just thinking of Antonio's party," she said quietly, her eyes unfocused.

"Let's not go through that again. Please, let's not. Just forget it."

"What did you say?" She turned toward him. "What did you say? Forget it! How the fuck does one go about forgetting almost being raped? How?" She was rigid, taut as line, glaring at him. A bespectacled older man across the aisle turned from reading and lowered his jaw, looked at them from the top of his glasses and then sheepishly returned to his reading. Just then, the train lurched forward once, and then, moments later, once again.

The train was finally approaching the outskirts of Madrid.

Isabella met them at the station, explaining that Antonio was at a rehearsal for an upcoming concert in Malaga. He was a bassoonist with the Madrid Symphony Orchestra and had been with them for over a decade. She used to work as a kindergarten teacher but quit a few years previously when she developed lupus. Fortunately, the drugs she was taking now seemed to control the facial rash and the arthritis in her hands.

Isabella drove them to her apartment in a modest area of the city. After unpacking, Sergio dressed nattily, as usual, and left for a luncheon meeting with his editor. Anna and Isabella decided to eat at a nearby restaurant. Isabella was a chatterbox and Anna loved being with her.

Isabella was in her mid-forties, more than a decade older than Anna. She and Antonio had lost a child early in pregnancy several years after they were first married and, despite trying, she failed to become pregnant. Lately, they had been considering adoption, but they anticipated problems because of her health. Fortunately, Isabella was very close to her sister-in-law, Carmen, a social worker, so she discussed it with her by phone and got some information on adoption agencies. Carmen lived with her husband and three kids and the families saw each other often. When they did, Isabella loved playing with Nadia, her five-year old niece. Antonio was always pleased seeing Isabella on the floor playing with her, peeking into Nadia's favorite toy, a cardboard playhouse, and arranging tiny furniture and figures in the rooms. She just loved kids.

On the ride home, Isabella seemed unusually quiet, thinking, thinking that maybe she should get a surrogate mother to carry a child. A client of hers had done just that last year. She wondered what had happened. She wondered how one goes about contacting a potential surrogate. She remembered hearing some scary stories of some unscrupulous agencies. She reminded herself to speak to Carmen about it when she got home. Isabella mentioned the matter to Anna and asked her what she thought. Anna hesitated before answering, completely occupied with her own problems and maybe a possible solution.

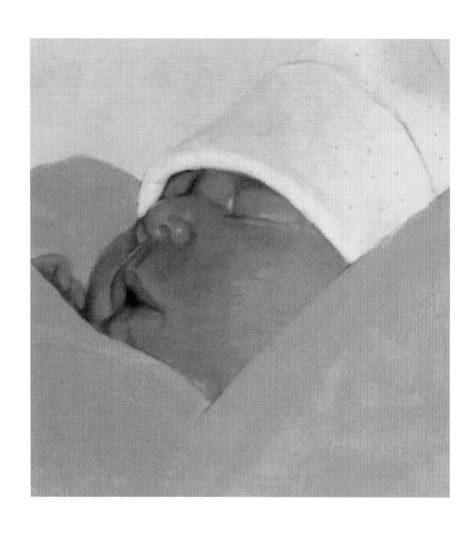

The Budding Artist And The Cherry Tree

I know something about art since I have painted for over fifty years. You'd think that I could teach my bright little granddaughter something about painting, wouldn't you?

I'm a serious artist, having sold scores of paintings and having exhibited in many galleries. I studied art everywhere I could, either at art schools or privately with well-known artists. I spent long hours experimenting with mixing colors in my studio and read scores of art magazines, thirsty for tidbits that might improve my work. Moreover, I love to teach art and have been teaching at a school in Florida where I recently retired.

From the time she could hold a pencil or a Crayola, Olivia always seemed hunched over some coloring book or sheet of paper, her nose hovering over her busy little right hand. She seemed obsessed. Of course, she played with her younger brother Grant and cared for her dolls, but, whenever Ilene and I traveled to Dallas, my son's home, she was drawing or painting. She had studied with a highly recommended children's art teacher for a while.

When she entered kindergarten, I wondered if I shouldn't try to teach her some elementary concepts of drawing. After all, she walked and talked early and by the age of five, she was reading.

But, of more importance, I wanted her to have a hobby that she could enjoy for the rest of her life. I hear retired friends grumble that they are bored because they have nothing to do. Often the reason is that they're physically unable to play golf or tennis because of injuries. Some even yearn to return to business. Even with most orthopedic

149

disabilities, artists can usually paint as long as they can see. Just think of Renoir who painted with a brush strapped to his severely arthritic fingers.

Last week, I glanced over my shoulder and saw Olivia sitting at the kitchen table. She had drawn a man next to a house together with the mandatory happy yellow sun with its radiating spokes. I studied the work for a while and was really impressed. Sure, it looked like a child's drawing, but I sensed something strong and solid about it. Of course, I wanted to. I had seen children's work in books and posters, but this was really a little different. Olivia neatly colored in the grassy area surrounding the man and the house and barely encroached on the outlines of either. As I shifted my gaze to her face, I saw that her eyes were squinting and her tongue had crept out of its cozy home and had migrated to her upper lip. She was so completely involved in her work that she didn't hear me ask if I might suggest something to improve her art.

"Olivia, might grandpa Richie suggest something?" I asked her. There was no answer at first, so I repeated the offer. She then turned her head toward me. Her light, blue-colored eyes opened wide and her long, scraggly, brown hair drooped haphazardly in strands. She didn't seem too happy.

"Al-l-l right, Grandpa. What is it?' she said.

I began to feel that I was making a mistake. Lately, my son had put her in time out more frequently than her brother because she was getting a little sassy. I hesitated giving her my suggestion, but couldn't control myself.

"Olivia, don't you think the man is a little tall for the house? How could he possibly fit through the door?"

Olivia didn't answer me. She just swiveled her head back to her drawing, hunched over again and acted as if I had said nothing or was not actually in the room with her. There was silence.

Suddenly, she bolted from her chair, looked me straight in the face, her arms akimbo and her legs spread far apart. "Grandpa, don't you think there are some very tall people in the world?"

I knew where that came from. My son is a basketball nut and takes both kids to Maverick games. But wait. Hadn't I seen a photograph taken by Diane Arbus of an almost eight-foot son towering over his bewildered parents who were huddling to one side of their small Bronx apartment? The giant's head almost reached the ceiling! I knew she was not aware of the picture, but, momentarily, I felt like a fraud.

"Besides, Grandpa," she added, "there *are* some artists who have to use their imagination and don't listen to teachers all the time!"

I could not believe this conversation was taking place. Was I dreaming?

"Well, sure there are, but..." I started to think twice before I said anything further. Maybe I should let her work at her own pace, After all, there were famous artists who were self-taught and never took a lesson?

"I like the way you drew the man and the house." I said humbly.

I felt defeated. Me, the guy who listens to classic music, attends serious courses on international affairs and who has life experience, struggling with her intellectually? Talk about asymmetrical warfare! I walked into the living room, sat down and pondered my situation further.

I recalled that just the other day, my wife told me something about herself when she was a young camper. We were at the Metropolitan looking as some of Grandma Moses' paintings when Ilene said that her first cousin was a junior counselor who taught arts-and-crafts at a camp in the Adirondacks. He was trying to teach her how to paint a cherry tree. Arnold was a talented 14-year old who had just been accepted at the prestigious "School of Music and Art." Ilene had put cherries all over the leaves of the tree and he was telling her, correctly, to mass in all the leaves first, and then gingerly put in a cherry here and there. Doing it that way would make the cherry tree more real. He showed her exactly how to do it and left. Almost immediately, Ilene put back the cherries, even more than before.

The Innocent Killer

Morris Minsky was both a schlemiel and a schlemazil. He was the guy who always knocked over the Manischewitz barely moments after everyone sat down at seders. Naturally, when hot soup was spilled accidentally at restaurants or at home, it always fell on him.

Minsky worked as a salesman in a town near Sing Sing prison in upstate New York. The store he worked in was called Sing Sing Petorama. He was a whiz at selling canaries from Papua New Guinea, although he also wasn't bad with Brazilian parrots and Madagascan macaws. He knew that he was reduced to having this menial job because he was a bungler who was awful at giving change to customers or remembering telephone numbers.

Minsky didn't make much money, but for a single guy who shared the rent on a small apartment with an older roommate, Mandelbaum, a starving artist, he was able to get by. Mandelbaum worked part time in a bagel store in town, dipping the annular pieces of wet dough into bowls of sesame or poppy seeds.

Minsky had never visited the prison, but was aware of the terrible people housed there by the guards who visited the store. Just the thought of the inmates scared the wits out of him. He often wondered why anyone would commit a crime and risk being confined for years, or, God forbid, life, in such a stony fortress.

After work, he would bicycle home and have dinner with Mandelbaum. The artist seldom spoke and always had a sad look on his face, like people plagued with painful corns or bunions.

For dinner, Minsky would often gorge himself on an inexpensive can of Heinz Boston Baked Beans. His boss never realized that the noxious smell that intermittently stunk up the little store was from Minsky because the disgusting odor of bird shit was stronger.

At meals with Mandelbaum, Minsky repeatedly spoke of his boring work in the store. Mandelbaum tried to interest him in painting, but Minsky just shook his head sideways. He had a hobby of his own —writing comedic short stories.

"How's that large painting going?" Minsky asked the artist one evening.

"Not well. Not well at all, Morris. Believe me, this is a tough way to earn a living."

After dinner, Mandelbaum went to his easel and Minsky started to type on his old Smith-Corona typewriter. Because they worked side by side in their small apartment, Mandelbaum soon noticed that Morris was flinging more and more crumpled sheets of paper into the wastepaper basket that sat between them. Not only did the writer seem dejected, but he also took deep sighing breaths and mumbled dirty words.

Mandelbaum had his own problems. He was struggling with his painting and it was getting the best of him. He favored beach scenes of children. The pictures always included a profusion of colorful designs on bathing suits; he would spend hours working on the details of the design, putting less effort into painting the ocean and the sky. He found it odd that the painting he was working on the night before looked worse then he remembered. Unbeknownst to him, Minsky accidentally knocked over the painting in the middle of the night when he went to pee. He wiped the paint off the floor and returned the painting to the easel. The klutz couldn't bring himself to tell the artist what happened. Mandelbaum thought the painting was really, really bad and he needed help with it. He thought of his old teacher, Marcello, a successful painter living in the city. Mandelbaum decided to visit Marecello with the painting the next day and seek advice.

Minsky didn't have writer's block as Mandelbaum suspected. Ideas for stories filled the nebish's mind. His characters were all well thought out and interesting. He memorized and did most of the things that he was taught in his creative writing classes. His funny stories usually had a protagonist, antagonist and a catalyst and always reached a climax. His mind wandered. Climax...Sex...Mimi!

Mimi was his girlfriend for the past year and she was great in bed. He loved her and wanted to marry her. He had met her parents some time ago when the West Virginians visited her. Minsky liked them. Mimi's father was a miner and loved talking to Morris on a topic that was as dear to both of them as it was to the prison guards—canaries. The father encouraged Mimi to marry him. After all, she was not good looking, had no chin and was getting older. Sure, Minsky was over forty, but the spinster was not far behind.

Before he returned to his writing, Minsky remembered that the previous week, when Mimi came to his apartment, she had threatened to leave him if he didn't make some type of commitment, or, more important, at least give her an engagement ring. She cried and cried. They both knew that the problem was the pet store job---it paid peanuts.

"Mimi, I know that I just have to sell some stories and make some real money. I know that. I just get these depressing rejection slips. I already have a huge pile of them on my desk," he said, pointing to them.

He was beside himself. He didn't know what to do.

Late in the afternoon, Mandelbaum returned from discussing his problems with Marcello. He seemed happy but said very little. He wolfed down his dinner and hurried to his easel to work on the painting that he had schlepped to Marcello.

Minsky sat at his typewriter, thinking that it would help a lot if he could afford a computer, maybe a brighter lamp or maybe even an old edition of the OED. He started to write but heard a screeching sound that he had never heard before. He glanced over at Mandelbaum and saw something odd. The artist had a palate knife in his right hand and was scraping paint off a small area of his painting. Minsky had no idea what was going on, because, in a short while, the otherwise dour Mandelbaum began to whistle and actually began to smile.

"Mandelbaum, what's going on? You're scraping down some of the painting. All that hard work, and you're destroying it?"

"I know. I know. Marcello's responsible. He told me that the intricate patterns I put on the bathing suit were well done—very, very well done---but the excessive detail didn't fit in with the mood of the rest of the painting. I spent too much time on unimportant detail. Scrape it away and redo it so it fits with the painting as a whole. *'Kill your babies,'* he said, just before I left. 'Kill your babies.' "

"Wow," said Minsky. "Kill your babies!"

"Yeah, but look at the painting now. Look at how much better it is, Morris. I love it."

Minsky walked over and studied the painting. He scrutinized it up close and then, like some type of serious art critic, walked back from it and hunched over, peering and squinting at the beach scene. Mandelbaum never saw him take so much interest in his work.

"Mandelbaum," screamed Minsky, "It's great. Just great. I feel like I'm at the beach. I can almost smell the salt air." Morris smiled and lovingly patted his roommate's shoulder.

Mandelbaum said that he still had to do more with the painting before he would sign it, but he was thinking that the work really could be sold. It definitely was his best work. His whistling got louder.

A few days later, the artist realized that the writer was tossing even more sheets of paper into the wastebasket. Some were almost completely crumpled into tiny balls. Besides, Minsky was typing at breakneck speed. The constant tapping was actually bothering Mandelbaum.

"Morris, what's with you? Are you OK?"

Minsky didn't respond at first. He seemed like someone had hypnotized him.

"Mandelbaum, I started to think about what Marcello told you. You know that stuff about killing babies. I realized that I was having the same problem as you, falling in love with particular passages. I was afraid to tamper with them also. Now that I know better, I can see that my work is better. Much better," he shouted excitedly to Mandelbaum.

Minsky couldn't wait till he called Mimi and told her about his new revelation. He couldn't wait to see her and have her read his recast stories. He became manic and began mumbling to himself. He thought of submitting stuff to The New Yorker since they always publish funny short stories. He fantasized becoming famous like James Thurber. And, he also fantasized about being married to Mimi. He rushed to the phone to call her. He couldn't wait till she answered. His heart jumped when someone picked up the receiver.

"Mimi. Mimi. I did it. I did it. I killed my babies. I killed my babies!"

"Hello? Hello? Who is this?" an elderly woman asked.

"Mimi. Is that you?"

"No, this isn't Mimi. Who are you? Are you some type of nut? Killing your babies. Who the hell is speaking? I'm going to call the police. A madman like you should be locked up in Sing Sing...for life!"

The Art Show

I'm sure that my ability to draw well must be genetically related to the artistic talents of several of my mother's six oddball sisters. Sally designed hats and often decorated them with colorful flowers. Helen painted watercolors of mice. Molly loved drawing toenails.

I also drew because I had no siblings to play with. My father worked from dawn to dusk in a second-hand clothing store in mid-town. Mother often helped him out. Things were tough then as America was still reeling from the Depression.

I was a mediocre student at The Bronx High School of Science, getting by mainly because I was a grind. I think I was bright enough, but my artistic eye frequently impeded me from listening to what people were saying. If a teacher had a large nose, cauliflower ears or an underdeveloped chin, I studied the deformities, neglecting the teacher's words. I daydreamed a lot, imagining success and fame in a wide range of challenges. The one thing I really enjoyed was drawing. I drew cartoons for the school newspaper and spent free time in the Art Department making posters and doing whatever Mr. Kurzband asked. I had absolutely no trouble concentrating when I was creative.

Art languished while I went away to college and then to medical school. After I married though, I decided to take art classes but was limited by the demands of my family and my new dermatological practice. Because of my obsession, however, I squeezed some classes in at The Art Student's League.

I painted at home in a corner of our bedroom and slowly my work improved. I covered the walls of my waiting room with some of my paintings and sold a few to patients. Sometimes the transaction proved uncomfortable because patients often haggled. I sensed there was something unprofessional about the whole thing, particularly when one patient purchased a landscape and wanted me to rename it "Acne," allowing him to claim the cost as a medical expense since he was writing a check to his dermatologist.

I had a few shows, sold work outside my office and occasionally painted on commission. I enjoyed being an artist almost as much as being a dermatologist. I once overheard a patient waiting to have a facial growth removed, confide to my nurse that she loved that I was an artist and a dermatologist because, she reasoned, if he can create such detailed and accurate pictures, he must have a steady hand.

Eight years ago, after almost forty years of practice, I purchased a home with a studio in a community in Jupiter, Florida. I now divide my time equally between that home and another up north in Westhampton Beach that I occupy in the summer. I live in sunny areas year-round and wonder sometimes if my environment isn't a metaphor for my life.

But, early last spring, dark clouds appeared.

I had just seen an exhibit of abstract paintings in a gallery at Florida Atlantic University, an Honors' College near my home. I contacted the Head of the Art Department, Mary Austin, a pleasant woman in her sixties, and asked her if she would be interested in viewing my work for a possible show. "Sure," she replied, "Just send me slides of your paintings."

Almost immediately, I assembled a dozen slides and sent them to her. I waited anxiously for her reply. She called the following month, informing me that my work was accepted, but said that the school wanted paintings with much larger measurements than I sent her in a cover letter. In addition, I was admonished not to show giclée prints. Reasonable requests, I thought. A convenient month for the show, March, ten months away, was agreed upon. Even though the exact date for the show was not decided, I was delighted.

After I returned north, I purchased large canvases and filbert brushes and about a dozen tubes of acrylic paint. Instead of playing some golf or going to the beach, I worked indoors all summer, enlarging and improving many of my paintings, and creating several new ones. While I was assembling my collection, I realized that maybe I should do something different and more challenging since, besides young college students, people likely to visit the show would come from my retirement community and most had college degrees and more. Many were also likely to be enrolled in the nearby Lifetime Learning Society that was on campus. I decided to take digital photographs of my work, at intervals, as the paintings progressed, and display the resulting prints alongside the paintings. Moreover, I decided to accompany the photographs and the paintings with pertinent commentary. I imagined creating a different type of art experience for the viewer, one that would be praised as an example of what an art exhibit should be like. My old grandiose visions reappeared. I couldn't wait till March.

In early October, at great expense, I had all of the paintings shipped to Florida and after my wife and I arrived, I called Ms. Austin, to inquire about the exact date of the opening. The abstract artist whose exhibit at the university first triggered my interest had forewarned me that Ms. Austin had procrastinated about her opening date. I knew that my son and his family in Dallas, as well as my daughter in New York, were intent on coming to the show and I wanted to be sure that they would get plane reservations far in advance because March is probably the busiest season for flights to Florida.

"We have a slight problem," Ms. Austin said.

My heart sank as I heard her foreboding words. "The multiple hurricanes in Florida this year have damaged some of the campus buildings and one of them contains the gallery. Remember, the University is partially a state school, so repairs often become bureaucratic nightmares. But, I do think that sometime in March should still be our goal." Ms. Austin ended by apologizing, but the words seemed meaningless, much like the wasted words of some of my teachers when I was daydreaming.

I was more than upset, but quickly realized that there was nothing I could do but go ahead and continue preparing for the exhibit. It seemed reasonable to me that the school was probably more anxious to get the repairs finished than I was.

I refocused my energies on the task of creating a top-notch exhibit. I wrote and rewrote my comments about the paintings so that they would be crystal clear and contain no artistic jargon. I learned Photoshop to improve my prints.

I was fully occupied for the next month or so, but, although cautiously optimistic, I was definitely on edge.

The severest blow to my optimism came late in December when I called Ms.Austin again, but not before incessantly debating in my mind the pros and cons of *when* exactly to call. Ms. Austin always seemed pleasant when we spoke on the phone and I liked her, but what she was to say now was devastating. "The leak has not been fixed, but there's another problem. The University now requires that the newly formed *Art Committee* review all exhibits. I'm going to mail you a formal application. Please fill it out and return it as soon as you can. You won't have to send new slides. I'm sorry about the mix-up, but there's nothing I can do about it."

What? What? I was infuriated beyond belief.

I barely heard anything she said but "Art Committee! "Art Committee! ART COMMITTEE!" Didn't Ms. Austin tell me that I would have a show? Is this a way to run a University? I couldn't believe this was happening.

Life for the next few days revolved around eating--I think I gained three pounds in three days—and sleeping.

As I mulled over my situation, I realized that I had a losing hand, that Ms. Austin had aces and kings and I had threes and fours. I was forced to conclude that there was nothing to do but wait till the committee made up its mind.

I was really pissed because, after all, they not only had promised me the show, but I had gone to greater expense than I anticipated to prepare for it; the framing and shipping cost a bundle. And now, there may be no show? All that time up north, wasted, absolutely wasted, imprisoned in my studio, in what turned out to be a glorious summer! Of course, deep down, I realized that I didn't really "waste" the summer since I loved painting and the finished pieces really looked quite good. Unfortunately, I was so filled with rage that my thinking was out of whack.

I then realized that there was an even bigger problem. What exactly was I to do now? Should I continue further refining details of my work? Should I still rewrite and rewrite? I knew that overworking anything creative could be disastrous. Aren't those first few thoughts of a writer the precious ones, the ones with the most punch and emotional truth? And what about the prints? I probably could improve them further, but I was getting tired of looking at them.

I discussed the problem with my wife. She concluded, and I eventually agreed, that it was probably wisest to continue as if the show was to take place in March. After all, someone, some committee of sorts, had approved of my work previously. Wouldn't it be likely that they would also be on the newly formed Art Committee?

"Cheer up, I told myself. But, I couldn't, and not a day went by for the next several weeks that I didn't rush to pick up the mail as soon as it was delivered. I also was the first to answer the phone. Before I knew it, 2004 was gone.

In early January, not one peep was heard from my adversary. I picked up the phone twice to call but I barely heard a dial tone before I pressed "OFF."

Late in January, actually January 25th at 4:34, after returning from Michael's with some art supplies and from the pharmacy with more tranquilizers, my wife greeted me at the garage door.

"She called. Everything's fine. The show is on for March. The eight of March will be the opening."

"Why didn't you call me on my cell phone and tell me immediately? You know how upset I am about this whole thing?"

"I really wanted to see your face when you heard the good news."

Well, she got an eyeful, and an earful, too. I not only smiled broadly, but I let out a feral cry, a roar loud enough to wake up the entire elderly neighborhood of my gated community. I didn't care. They won't remember me anyway. I've been isolated in my studio, monk-like, for more than a year. Moreover, as everybody knows, the aged lose recent memory like car keys. And, they're also hard of hearing.

The "opening" for the exhibit lasted till about eight in the evening. I was surprised that the show was less crowded than I anticipated because I had mailed out scores of invitations. Searching for the exact addresses of friends—who normally puts ZIP codes in an address book? --is always a laborious task. From past experience, I should have been prepared for the meager attendance. It's trying to tell me something that I don't think I want to hear.

As Ilene and I left the building with my family and few good friends, I wondered if the show was worth all the trouble. After all, although I love painting, I labored for almost two years and I had plenty of angst. As best as I tried, I still couldn't help shoving some social obligations to the side. But, on the other hand, when it comes to shows, being a painter or even a writer, is far preferable to being an actor or a musician. Just think of it. A painter or sculptor works on a forthcoming "performance" and when he or she finishes creating the work, it's done. The artist goes to the opening, the writer goes to the signing and both usually enjoy a pleasant social experience without the anxiety associated with performing further. That's not like a musician or an actor who have to "create" every night, sometimes once, but often for weeks or even years. I like being an artist.

The exhibit was in the main entrance hall of the University and remained there for about seven weeks. I'm sure it was glanced at by multitasking college students and faculty, maybe a hundred people at the most though, rushing to and from classes or social engagements. I have watched people at galleries and their attention spans are invariably brief, sometimes maybe a minute or so at maximum, incredible as that may seem. A minute or so. Socializing at shows always trumps serious looking.

Of course, having a museum show would have been a real high, but it is rarely realized by any of the estimated twenty-five million "artists" in the United States. Such a plum allows a huge audience to see your work. To me, and I imagine for any visual artist, that exposure is the most gratifying reward of creativity. You want as many people as possible to see your work. Imagine an artist or a writer toiling for years without anyone seeing anything they've done. No one at all! Imagine laboring for years writing a novel that is never read by anyone but maybe a few family members or friends?

I spent about three hours at the exhibit, schmoozing with friends and meeting a few new people. Ms. Austin was pleasant enough, but I sensed that she wanted to avoid me.

It is very difficult for any creative person to gauge the impression viewers have about their work of art. Probably, the only reliable indicator of approval is a sale or a positive review by a critic. Compliments from family, friends or strangers, while welcome, are always suspect to me. But, keep them coming.

Minnie

For several years, every Wednesday morning, I taught painting and drawing at an art school in Florida. I had retired to the state after almost 40 years of practicing dermatology and lived with my wife and small Tibetan terrier in a gated-community nearby. During the half-hour ride to work, I thought about the previous week's class and how to improve my teaching. The students were mainly elderly women since Wednesdays were traditionally men's golfing days at the many clubs peppering the area.

Approaching the one-story, ochre-colored building, I noticed a white Mercedes parked near the entrance. I knew all the cars the student's drove because I usually arrived a little late. I realized that the car probably belonged to the new student who had called earlier in the week to inquire about the class. She sounded quite young. She had questioned me closely about whether there were comfortable chairs in the studio. Most students stand while painting, although some, myself included, prefer sitting. Still, I wondered about the question.

As I entered the classroom, students were setting up for the morning's work. A small woman, her gray hair tied in a tight bun, sitting with her back to me, a red cane hooked onto the back of her chair, was obviously the new student. A square amber-colored bottle stood nearby on the floor. The bottle caught my eye because it had a black label reminding me of Jack Daniels bourbon. I ignored it while I gathered my thoughts on a demonstration that I usually gave at the beginning of each class.

An attractive, redheaded woman, holding a manila envelope, was standing beside the older woman. She turned and approached me, but the seated woman seemed preoccupied with something in her lap.

"Hi. I'm Minnie Mahoney's companion," Anne Finnegan said, pointing to the elderly woman. "I was the one who spoke to you last week."

"Oh, yes. I remember. You also inquired about the chair. I assume that Ms. Mahoney is the student, not you."

She nodded in agreement. "By the way, she prefers being called 'Minnie,' not Ms. Mahoney," Ann added.

"Fine," I said. "I like informality."

Ann walked over to Minnie, tapped her shoulder, bent over and whispered, "Minnie, Richard, the teacher, is here."

The elderly woman turned around slowly and smiled. She was holding a sketchpad and there were pencils and a kneaded eraser lying on the table next to her. She looked to be in her seventies or eighties and was round-shouldered and her face was wrinkled, but when she smiled, I sensed that she must have been pretty when she was young. We chatted briefly. She told me that she felt a little anxious going to school at her age, but that she loved to draw. She just regretted never taking lessons. She winced now and then and held her left knee. It was obvious that she had arthritis in her knees. She tried to have them replaced, she said, but her orthopedist told her she was too old. That infuriated her and she decided she was going to find another orthopedist. Anne told me later, that Minnie's overall health was remarkably good. She added that Minnie was a spiritual person who was convinced that someone was watching over her.

Ann whispered something into Minnie's ear and placed the manila envelope next to the pencils and eraser. She told me that she would be gone for an hour or so, leaving Minnie alone with the rest of the class.

"Just be sure that she drinks water now and then," she told me. "She has a tendency to get dehydrated and it causes her to become light headed."

Before she left, I asked Anne about the Jack Daniels. I felt sort of stupid asking the question and wondered for a moment if I had not read the label wrong. My eyesight was good, but not great.

Ann burst out laughing. "Richard. I'm so sorry. I forgot to warn you. Minnie has a great sense of humor. Oh, she'll just love it when I tell her how bewildered an expression you just had on your face when you asked about the bottle. That bottle of Jack Daniels has nothing in it but *Poland Spring water*! I should have Minnie tell you about the stunt she pulled off in college on a smart-ass, mathematics major. The evening before the girl was to go on vacation to Hawaii, Minnie sneaked into her empty room and stole her suitcase. She brought it to her adjacent dorm room and frantically opened it, removed the girl's clothing and replaced it with bags of garbage. Watch out for her, Richard.

The room was starting to buzz with activity and with the smell of turpentine. Because I always felt that a new student deserved priority, I pulled up a folding chair and sat down next to Minnie. She told me that the envelope contained a photograph and wanted to show it to me. It was of a young woman wearing a broad-brimmed, crocheted hat and a handsome burgundy and pale green shift who was sitting on a park bench with her hands in her lap. Minnie said she wanted to draw her. I often teach students to draw or paint from photographs rather than from a still-life set up or a model; it is definitely easier. Most contemporary realistic painters and, surprisingly, not an insignificant number of the Impressionists, painted from them. The evidence was often found after they died.

As we discussed the photograph, I gave her some hints about the initial drawing. She worried about doing the fingers and hands; students generally struggle with hands, especially the placement of the fingers, but I reassured her that I'd help with that if she needed it.

"Richard," she asked, "do you realize that the young woman in that picture was me? My husband took it in the Luxembourg Gardens when we were on our honeymoon in Paris. My God, it was so long ago. I can't believe it. He's been gone for over twenty years." Her voice trailed off and I felt the need to say something, but nothing came out.

I tended to other students and then headed to an anteroom where Peggy, who ran the small school, had prepared coffee. She came over and sat next to me. "Richard, did you know that Minnie'll be *one hundred and three* in six weeks! One hundred and three! Isn't that amazing? Some friends are making a big deal of it and planning a party at town hall. The mayor wants Friday, April 30, her birthday, to be recognized as *Minnie Mahoney Day*. Her children, grandchildren and great grandchildren are coming. Photographers from the local paper are going to be there. She's apparently the oldest woman in the entire county. I was told that the Celebration Committee asked Minnie to exhibit one of her drawings since Anne had told them that she loved to draw. She had agreed. I think that's why Anne had encouraged Minnie to take my class."

Peggy was beside herself. She was normally business-like and unemotional, but this morning, she was giddy. I was a little light-headed myself. I had never taught anybody that old. I wondered if anybody had. I immediately thought *Guinness Book of Records*, or something like that, because if one was to consider the age of the student or even the *combined* age of the student and the teacher, it seemed to me it was unique. I was 76 at the time.

I returned to the studio thinking that I just wanted Minnie to have a good time. Light on the teaching, I thought. I was sure that I should have no other goal for someone her age. I first looked at the work of my other students, made suggestions about their drawings and about color or value for those who were painting. After about an hour, I returned to Minnie. Her beginning was fine, but the shape of the right hand was wrong. I sat down next to her and emphasized the good things she had done first, then, mentioned the hand and precisely what she could do to improve it. She nodded and seemed to understand. Just as I was about to get up and return to the other students, Minnie asked if it was OK if she stopped. She was a little tired and thirsty. At that moment, Anne returned to the studio and Minnie asked her to take her home. She was obviously tired and her voice was cracking a bit. In a few minutes, they were gone.

Peggy called me that afternoon and asked if she could give Anne my home telephone number because she wanted to speak to me about something. Why, not? Anne telephoned a few days later and said that Minnie was so enthusiastic about the drawing that she was skipping her midday nap to finish it. She thanked me for my help and then added, "Would it be alright if Minnie called you if she had any further problem with the hand?"

"Certainly," I said. "In fact, if she really has difficulty, I wouldn't mind going over to her house and seeing the work and then make suggestions. Tell her not to worry." I knew from house calls.

I cancelled class on April 15th because I had a miserable cold and laryngitis. I didn't want to infect anybody, especially a woman who was over 100. I was glad that neither Anne nor Minnie had called because I was in no mood to talk.

The next class was on April 22 and as I approached the school, I realized that I had not heard from Minnie and wondered why. I parked next to the white Mercedes. I was anxious to see what Minnie had done, but, unbeknownst to me, Anne had called Peggy late the previous evening, to say that Minnie was ill and wouldn't be coming in, but that she was almost finished with the drawing.

Peggy greeted me halfheartedly when I entered the school. Anne was standing next to her and had bad news scrawled all over her faces. Minnie had pneumonia and had a high fever. The local doctor had recommended that she be hospitalized. I knew pneumonia when it affected the elderly and my heart sank. As I struggled to say something reassuring, Anne's cell phone rang. She answered it and said it was the doctor as then scurried away.

The next day, Anne called me and said that Minnie had died. I had several patients who died from melanoma in my practice and it always shook me up. I felt the same way with Minnie although I had seen her only once.

The town decided to have the memorial for Minnie anyway, probably later the next month. She had completed the drawing and Anne called me and asked if I would meet her at the school early the next day so that I could see it before it was matted and framed.

There was no joy left in me as I drove to the school that morning. Anne had the drawing sitting on the table in the studio when I arrived. Minnie had done a good job in obtaining a likeness. Her hands were fine except for one thumb that was off a bit and the hat just didn't sit correctly on the head. My eyes were drawn to both errors almost immediately. Anne's cell phone rang while I was looking at Minnie's drawing. She seemed concerned when she spoke to the caller. She excused herself and said that she'd be on the phone for a little while. It was from Minnie's lawyer and had something to do with Minnie's estate.

Like a thief, I quickly went to the cabinet where my pencils, paints and brushes were stored and hurriedly plucked out an HB and 2B pencil and an eraser. Frantically, I corrected the thumb and the hat. I had never drawn or erased so quickly in my life. The drawing snapped into focus. I imagined I saw Minnie winking at me when I made the change, a mischievous smile developing over her face, signaling that she approved of my alteration. I suspect that she would have done the same for me.

When Anne finally returned, she glanced at the drawing and then at me, carefully looking me in the eye. I said nothing, just smiled conspiratorially, and thought of that little bottle of bourbon, the purloined suitcase and the delightful old woman who enlivened my life for just a few moments before she disappeared.

Twenty Bucks

Moskowitz loved to sculpt. As an only child, Arnie was always modeling Playdo, creating funny little men and women who always had matted spaghetti-like strands of clay for hair and a large nipple for a nose. Eyes were made by jabbing the eraser end of a lead pencil into the sides of the nose. His signature Martha-Ray mouth was created by lengthwise enlargement of a hole similar to that made for each eye. As he grew older, Moskowitz's parents paid for him to take art classes with an old man who taught in the cluttered basement of his Bronx home. Five of the other students were girls, and he wondered, but dared not ask, why none of his basketball friends were interested in art. He feared that they might think of him as a sissy. After only a few months of classes, his work improved and he dreamt of becoming a real sculptor. He was convinced that he would become famous and create masterpieces like the stone sculptures of Chester French.

He recalled his love for sculpting some 45 years later, soon after he retired from practicing plastic surgery in Manhattan, when his wife, Sylvia, mentioned that a local art school was offering sculpture classes.

"Arnie, maybe you should consider taking it up again? You're always complaining about the agita golf gives you and about the pain in your knees when you play tennis." Sylvia handed him the "Arts and Leisure Section" of the local daily where the advertisement appeared. He studied it closely and agreed with her idea.

The school was a short drive from the gated community where he lived. When he entered its parking lot, he looked for a spot, but wondered why there was a white car parked perpendicular to the rear of several other cars. A black man was in the driver's seat, talking on a cell phone. The engine was not running, but the hood was up.

Moskowitz drove by the car and found a parking space, totally preoccupied with registering for the class and wondering what the other students and the teacher would be like.

The students in the class were all middle aged or elderly and all were women, except for a retired proctologist. They chatted amicably about the model and the physician's sculpture of him. The work was pretty good although Moskowitz thought the buttocks were grossly enlarged. He wondered what the work of a urologist would look like.

As soon as the class was over, Moskowitz hurried to his car because Sylvia had told him that they had to go to Home Depot and then to an early movie afterwards. They were forced to cancel the trip several times previously because of this or that reason.

Right after Arnold got into the driver's seat, he noticed that someone was approaching the car. He thought it was the same guy who was on his cell phone when Arnold originally entered the parking lot. The man appeared to be in his forties, slim, with a pleasant looking face and a slender black mustache. He was dressed in black slacks and a white shirt with a multicolored rep tie. He was wearing a broad-brimmed hat. He was speaking to someone on his cell phone as he approached, but Moskowitz couldn't understand what he was saying. The stranger seemed a bit agitated. He obviously wanted to speak to Arnold since he approached the car from the driver's side. Moskowitz rolled down his window and tensed up.

"Sorry to bother you, but my battery's dead, and I can't start my car. I've been on the phone for hours, pleading with friends for help, but everybody is at work or otherwise unavailable. Do you have jumper cables?" He spoke English well but with a slight French accent and Moskowitz wondered if he might be from Haiti or The Dominican Republic.

Arnie actually had a jumper cable in the trunk. It was jammed into a nylon traveling bag together with other emergency supplies like a flashlight, a bungee cord and an aerosol can of air in case he got a flat.

He was about to get out of his car and get the cable, when he began to have reservations. Who was this guy? Why had he *really* been in the parking lot for hours? He wondered if this was some type of scam like the one that happened to him as he left Rueben's delicatessen in midtown a few years prior. A black man in a baggy raincoat, who was wearing a baseball cap, had suckered him into a ruse. He was blocking Arnold's path, bending over and obviously searching for something on the sidewalk.

"I lost my contact lens. Could you help me find it?" the man asked Arnold. Moskowitz stooped to help the poor guy since he himself wore contacts. Just then, he heard Sylvia scream, "Get out of there! Stop! Police!" An accomplice was dipping his hand into Arnold's wallet pocket. Hearing his wife's screams, both plotters disappeared into the midtown crowd.

He had also succumbed to a mustard scam last year when a black guy offered to remove the condiment from Arnold's jacket while an accomplice tried to steal his wallet.

Moskowitz was a bleeding-heart liberal. He grew up in a home where strong labor unions were admired, where FDR was revered and where a frequent topic of conversation on Sundays, when many of his Bronx relatives met to play poker, eat a little strudel and drink some hot tea, was civil rights. He berated friends and relatives if they dare say *schwartza* when *blacks* would be just fine.

"I don't have a jumper cable!" Moskowitz answered, as he glanced around the lot for a possible accomplice.

The stranger saddened and returned to his car, slowly opened the door and sank back in the driver's seat.

Arnie felt awful.

Why the hell did I lie? he wondered. If I had given him the cable, the whole thing would be done by now. He began to have that same mounting anxiety and breathlessness that he often experienced when he first began doing dermatological surgery and encountered complications. He pondered whether he would have helped him if he were white.

Moskowitz drove to the man's car, opened his passenger-side window, and shouted to the stranger. The man was on his cell phone again, but put it down and opened his window.

"Let me call my brother-in-law and see if he can help," Moskowitz said.

"Great," said the stranger.

Herbie was home and said he couldn't come for a few hours because he was trying to repair a broken screen door. Arnold realized that that was not good enough. Sylvia would plotz if he cancelled on her again.

"I have an important appointment in half an hour," the stranger said. "I was thinking that I might even try to walk there but I'm preventing two cars from backing up if I leave."

Moskowitz began to realize that this guy might just be the genuine article. After all, his car was an Acura. Besides, he was better dressed then Arnold. Moskowitz was tempted to ask him about his appointment and where it was and where he worked, but as he started to, a wild, probably unwise, thought popped into his head.

"Look," Moskowitz suggested, "why don't I get a couple of the guys at the school to move your car so it's not blocking anyone. We'll leave a note on your windshield saying that the battery is dead, but the driver will return shortly. After you get back from your appointment, try your friends again. Wait here. I'll get some help. I'm sure I'll get you to your appointment on time. I'll drive you if I have to!" Moskowitz couldn't believe he made the offer.

The surprised man thanked Arnold and shook his head up and down and said, "Great. That would just be great." Arnold hurried back to the school and returned with two students and they all succeeded in moving the car to the side. As he headed out of the lot, with the man in the passenger seat, Arnold noticed that he put his safety belt on. The act reassured him.

They drove north and turned right after two blocks. The odd couple spoke only about how to get to the stranger's destination.

"Now turn left at Clover Street, just beyond the Exxon station on the right, and we won't be far from the courthouse," the passenger instructed.

Courthouse! Courthouse! Arnold's pulse became irregular and he became a little dizzy. He had images of Sylvia and his buddies Lipshitz and Abramowitz laughing in disbelief as he told them what happened. He almost heard the word *schmuck* and the phrase "Were you out of your fucking mind?" He imagined the story as it would appear somewhere on the back pages of the Palm Beach Post if this strange encounter terminated tragically.

"There it is! Over there, just beyond the supermarket," the stranger exulted. Moskowitz asked him how he would get back to his car later. He said he would walk. He didn't have enough money on him to take a taxi and public transportation was not available.

Arnold pulled up to the courthouse. Cops and lawyerly types with heavy briefcases were hurriedly walking up or down the steps of the massive white building. Cars with license plates containing few letters were parked in spaces next to signs that read "Official Cars Only." Relieved that he wasn't dead and guilty that he challenged the honesty of the stranger, Moskowitz excitedly pulled out a twenty from his wallet and gave it to him. "Here. This should take care of the taxi!"

The recipient looked at Moskowitz. He then looked down at the money, took it, and exited the car as calmly as he entered. He never turned around, but disappeared through a revolving door at the top of the stairs.

Arnold felt good, real good.

The Man With The World's Best Memory

Morris Moskowitz died last week while he was eating. He loved stuffing himself with Molly's greasy and unhealthy meals. He was seated, stooped over and devouring a capacious bowl of her chicken soup with kreplach when it happened. At the same time as he was eating, he was eying the rest of the dinner table like a wild animal searching for some appetizing prey. His forehead was sweating from the hot soup. He could see, just beyond the gilded rim of the soup bowl, that Molly was ladling pot roast for him onto a huge platter, planning to abut the meat against a mountain of buttered mashed potatoes already occupying almost half the plate's acreage. Man, was he hungry! Suddenly, he lurched forward, hitting his bald pate against the edge of the table, and gasping and uttering something about... *more gravy*! He slid onto the floor in one loud plop, his chair falling backward. A random kreplach rolled silently off the table and bounced off the chair onto his head. Two-hundred, sixty-three pounds died, just like that, in an instant. You'd think that the fatter you are, the longer it would take for you to die.

Everybody who knew Moskowitz loved him. Not only was he likeable, but he also had an incredible memory. For sure, anybody who conversed with him, however briefly, never forgot his ability to pluck arcane facts from nowhere. His gift was better than that Ken guy on "Jeopardy." He probably acquired the skill from his parents who were both history professors. The elder Moskowitz's were also movie buffs who had seen and often discussed scores of films since they were first married, a love he acquired when he got older.

Moskowitz and his best friend, Solly, both worked in mid-town. Moskowitz was an actuary and Solly worked in a rip-off gift shop on Fifth Avenue. For years, they had lunched together on Saturdays at a luncheonette in mid-town. Their wives played canasta together all afternoon.

It was at the luncheonette that Moskowitz first told Solly about his earliest memories as a child. Until then, Mosk had astounded him with the names of tiny towns in Lithuania, the details of meals they ate together a decade ago in Longchamps--he even remembered how much they tipped!--and all the statistics on all sorts of football and basketball games and players.

Solly will never forget what Moskowitz said just a few days before he died. They had just finished lunch.

"Solly, do you know that I still remember the color of the crib I slept in," he began. "I even remember the designs and colors of my father's ties, but, what amazes even me, is that---are you ready, Solly?--- I still remember my last few days in my mother's womb and, even, my birth."

After unleashing these rather incredible revelations, Moskowitz sat back in his chair like some big shot poker player with a handful of aces. He tilted his head up and down and overlapped his lower lip on the upper. Then, he silently slid his gold toothpick between his two back teeth and worked it until a fleck of sour pickle was extracted. He stared at his catch and said nothing. There was a faint smile on his face.

"Moskowitz, what the hell are you talking about? Nobody remembers things about their birth. Nobody! What, are you nuts? I think they say that the furthest back that we can remember is when we were about three, maybe four. But, *our birth?* No way. Hey. What you smoking friend?"

"Solly. I even remember my last days in mom's womb. I remember floating freely in dark smelly water. Every now and then, I collided with a wall, but just as easily, I was able to float away, like an astronaut. I realized I was tethered by a cord to a small mound on her womb and could touch the cord, but couldn't grab it because it was so slippery. It became like a game to me, trying to grip the fucking cord. It was weird. I couldn't see anything; only heard Shirley's heart beat.

Solly had had it. He was always jealous of Morris's memory and lost a bundle on wagers, but this crap about his fetal memories got to him. He decided that he would bet Moskowitz on his memory and grabbed for his back pant's pocket, fleshed out his wallet and carefully picked out fifty bucks.

"Here, Morris, fifty dollars. I bet you're lying. I don't believe anything you said. Put up or shut up," he threw the dough down, some of the money falling on a plate of half-eaten coleslaw.

"Solly. Wait a while. I can't prove that shit about my mom's pregnancy and you know it, but I swear to you, I remember it all. Solly. Have I ever lied to you?"

Solly thought for a moment and agreed. As far back as he remembered, Moskowitz never lied, even in stickball games or in pool. Never even about broads.

"Mosk, you're right. Forget the bet." He sounded defeated, but deep down he was suspicious. The stuff was too outlandish.

Moskowitz offered to tell Solly about his first few years of life, but Solly begged off. He had enough.

They finished their lunch and decided to see a movie. They bought a Post and looked up the movie schedule, but they couldn't agree on what to see. Solly noted that *Symphony Space* was having a Charles Laughton festival and he loved him. "Moskowitz, they're playing 'Island of Lost Souls.' Have you seen it?"

"Sort of. That was a film mom and dad saw one night when I was about a year old. They discussed it at breakfast the next morning. I was in my white crib while they were having breakfast. Mom had just fed me Gerber's Apricot sauce."

"OK. OK, Mr. genius. You really remember what they said about the movie? Really?"

"Everything! Absolutely everything."

"Bullshit!"

"Solly. Just listen. The movie's a horror classic made in 1932. It was inspired by an H.G.Wells's story. Charles Laughton played a demented Dr.Moreau who tries to alter animals into human beings. The movie also starred Bela Lugosi, Richard Arlen, Kathleen Burk, Buster Crabb, Alan Ladd and, I think, Randolph Scott.

"Mosk, that's it. That's it. We're going over to the theatre and see the fucking movie."

They looked at the movie schedule and saw that they had to wait an hour or so before it began, so they decided to take a leisurely stroll up Broadway and pick up some candy before the show. They talked about how ridiculous and childish their arguments were and how, yes Solly accepted Mosk's memory as being terrific, but how Solly felt that he was being taken for a fool and it really pissed him off.

They saw the movie together, without even whispering anything to each other about Mosk's incredibly accurate memory of it. When the movie and the credits ended, Mosk got up first from his seat to go up the aisle, but realized that Solly was still sitting. And sitting. Mosk returned to him and Solly rose and followed Mosk out, both silent until they neared the exit.

"Mosk, we haven't been to Atlantic City for quite a while," Solly said." Let's do a little Twenty One, but instead of betting alone, we'll be partners."

The Ruckus

Once a year, Dr. Sam Brown visited his colleague, the ophthalmologist, Dr Arthur Rubin, for an eye examination. Art was Sam's undergraduate roommate at Duke and was the touchy-feely, artistic type who seemed least likely to end up in the sciences. But, oddly enough, he and Art were in the same class at The Johns Hopkins Medical School and have continued to keep in touch. They were both married and had kids.

Sam had a one-thirty appointment and, as usual with his appointments, arrived early. He played tennis the afternoon before and worked out for two hours the morning of his appointment.

Brown was accustomed to hard physical work and exercise. He retired in 1995 as a sport's orthopedist. He was often forced to stand for hours in the operating room, sawing through bones, and inserting all sorts of screws, plates and artificial joints in them, as well as lifting and holding up the muscular limbs of injured athletes, sometimes for hours. In addition, the six-foot-four Sam had dutifully exercised on a stationary bike for years. Sam was in good shape for a sixty-five-year old. He watched his diet and controlled his weight, which hovered around 170. The only thing Sam couldn't do was control his temper.

Sam entered a crowded waiting room and printed his name on a sheet of paper lying on a Lucite shelf in front of the secretary's window. He was wearing matching Fila tennis shorts and shirt. He was a good-looking guy with a Burt Lancaster face and a full head of wheat-colored hair.

Art's secretary appeared at the waiting-room window. She tilted forward, looked out of the opened, sliding-glass window and smiled benignly while her head swiveled to locate him.

"Dr. Brown? Dr. Brown? You can come in now," she said, pointing to him.

Sam looked at his watch. He was a bit irritated. It was already two fifteen. He was taken to a small room where a nurse tested his eye pressure and had him read the eye chart. Finally, she dripped fluid into both eyes to dilate his pupils and then handed him a pink tissue to wipe away any excess liquid. She then guided him to an adjacent room and disappeared.

Sam entered a narrow room and sat down. Conversation among patients and accompanying relatives or friends filled the room with a soft, modulated din. Most of the people were elderly. Soon after he sat down, Sam noticed a young couple enter. The woman sat on a chair next to Sam, and the man, carrying a container of coffee, sat next to her.

After a few moments, they started talking to each other. They spoke about Iraq and Sam disagreed with the man who was now speaking loudly. Sam listened to what they said and disliked the condescending way the man spoke to the woman.

The couple seemed oblivious to the other patients in the room, like people talking casually on cell phones in a crowded bus or train. They were probably both in their late twenties or early thirties, much younger than Sam; both were tanned, thin, and swarthy. From their conversation, Sam gleaned that the man's name was Frank and her name was Rose. Frank was wearing a tan peaked cap, had a well-trimmed mustache and appeared to have a full head of black hair. He was dressed warmly for Florida in a sweater, a jacket and long pants but it had been a cool day. He took off the sweater after a while and underneath he had a dark-blue, T-shirt emblazoned in front with the image of a basketball with *Knicks* printed in boldface orange beneath the ball. Sam was a fanatical fan of the Miami Heat, long-standing, bitter rivals of the Knicks. He *really* didn't like the guy.

Rose—Sam judged her to be the man's unfortunate wife—was pleasant looking with black, frizzy hair, a Barbie-doll nose, and sad, small, brown eyes that suggested she was just about ready to cry. She continued her discussions with Frank, all the while absentmindedly turning the pages of a very outdated copy of Art News which she had draped over her thighs.

Frank started to complain to Rose about overbooking by doctors. Sam could swear he also heard them talk about the *rip-offs* doctors committed and the *exorbitant fees* they charged. He was furious, but was distracted when the nurse entered the room and called out Sam's name. At last, he thought, looking at his watch. As Sam rose to exit the room with the nurse, Frank also rose, grabbed the nurse's forearm and informed her that *he* had arrived before Sam.

"What? What did you say?" roared Sam, as he turned to confront Frank. I came in before you! You must be kidding---*you* came in before me? Ha!"

"What the Hell are you talking about? I *know* I came in before you," Frank said.

Rose tried to calm Frank down, but before she could talk, Sam's kettle boiled over and he roared "You son of a bitch! I'll show you who came in first!" A fight seemed imminent.

The seated patients, some with watery eyes barely open and unfocused from eye drops and some with mouths beginning to gape at the unfolding drama, all rose slowly, almost in tandem, one with a walker, another with a rickety, white cane, and started to scatter.

Soon the men began to scuffle in the center of the small room. The evacuees fled toward the door, bumped into each other, stumbled blindly into chairs and a small side table, but, miraculously, succeeded in successfully eluding the central melee, as water does when interrupted in its flow by a rock in the middle of a stream.

Sam squinted to see, grunted, and then wildly and repeatedly punched Frank. Their ensuing struggle lacked a clear winner until Sam was accidentally thrown onto Frank because he tripped over a walker dislodged from the trembling hands of one of the escaping seniors. Frank tumbled backwards and collapsed on top of Rose, who was still seated, too stunned to move. The younger gladiator fought fiercely, and, as he sank into Rose's lap, her chair suddenly collapsed. As Frank sank, he grabbed hold of Sam's crisp new Fila shirt and accidentally tore the fabric with his protruding Knick souvenir ring. Hearing the tear, and quickly glancing at his ripped tennis shirt, Sam roared loudly, "Son of a bitch!"

The hubbub had attracted the attention of the staff. They rushed into the room, but were thwarted in their attempts to enter by the mob blindly fleeing. Frank tried to right himself from his awkward position on Rose's lap, but Sam pounced on him in a desperate effort to cause harm. Finally, Sam was able to punch Frank in the face, near his left eye, drawing blood. A primal whelp, like the cry of a wounded animal, filled the emptied room. Frank was attempting to shield his left eye from further damage when Dr Rubin appeared at the door.

Art rushed to Frank and forcibly removed his trembling hands from his bloodied eye.

"Ann, come quickly! I think we may have a fractured orbital bone," Rubin screamed to his trusted nurse in an adjacent room. He was unaware that his old medical schoolmate was hovering behind him surrounded by worried members of the ophthalmologic staff.

An unsteady and terrified Frank was escorted to the office's operating-room suite. Rose, sobbing and appearing disoriented, looked angrily at Sam as she followed her husband out of the room.

Sam was totally bewildered. He stood in the doorway, not knowing what to do or where to go. Both bruised hands were pressing on his temples as he surveyed the room. The broken legs of Rose's chair were lying on top of someone's white purse. Magazines were scattered everywhere. An elderly man peeked into the room and reached under a nearby chair to retrieve a small, white, plastic shopping bag bulging with used-golf balls that he abandoned when he was forced to flee. He departed sheepishly with the bag, leaving some balls on the floor, and glanced furtively in Sam's direction. A broken pair of schlock, gilded sunglasses, unfortunately smashed in the fog of the war, lay forgotten under a chair.

What the Hell did you do? Jesus Christ, Sam, what did you do? he lamented to himself. He felt defeated. He had lost badly in tennis the previous day to an outright bum. He also realized that the fight had aggravated his recently repaired rotator cuff and he was feeling some pain, but, worst of all, that son-of-a-bitch Frank, was seen by Art before he was!

A Cool Offer

MORRIS SHAPIRO
14 EAST 38th STREET
NEW YORK CITY 10018

OFFSHORE OFFICE: 91 SHADY LANE
CAYMAN ISLANDS

March 1, 2005

The Devil
1548 Netherworld Ave.
Hell, 76804

Dear Lucifer:

My name is Morris Shapiro. I represent Mr. Louis Ballbusta, the President of FreezaYoassoff Air-Conditioning Company, and am writing to you on a matter of extreme urgency. I have been a lawyer for over 30 years, although for seven years I was unable to practice because of a complicated and prolonged vacation of sorts. I received a B.A. degree from the University of Phoenix in 1965 and a law degree from a school in Somalia three years later.

Mr. Louis Ballbusta is a client of mine and he has been bothered by business conversations he has had with several of his customers who have suggested that "You should only go to Hell!" Recently, a metal fabricator terminated a very lucrative deal with the same disgusting suggestion. These expressions of dissatisfaction with Mr. Ballbuster's business dealings have prompted him to offer you an unusual and inexpensive air-conditioning contract. You should know that my client is very superstitious and takes the warnings he has been given very seriously because of ominous arrangements of calamari and scungilli in a pasta dish he ate many years ago.

Mr Ballbusta admits that he is easily angered. Perhaps he has even associated with men who one might deem undesirables and that fisticuffs were employed in situations where more discussions might have been fruitful. But, on the other hand, he is a deeply religious man who is good to his children, even to his dim-witted son, referred to by friends as "Creep," who works for the company crawling into and cleaning out brand new air-conditioning ducts.

Louis is deserving of a break. He worked as a young man for years in the garment district lugging huge stacks of boxes for dressmakers. He saved his money, lived frugally and through a good friend ended up being a minor partner of Freezayouassoff.

I know you must have enormous clout with your Admission's Committee, so I wonder if you could urge them to reject Mr. Ballbusta's admission, which Louis feels may be imminent.

If you reject his admission, Louis will agree to air condition any portion of your home or office. He also would like you to consider allowing his company to air condition the residences of some of his very close friends. After all, most of them really committed only questionable white-collar crimes, although admittedly, very occasionally, their felonies were accompanied by hematological incidents with unintended mortuarial consequences.

Top-of-the-line, air-conditioning units will be installed and the work will be done expeditiously. His usual 100-year maintenance contract would be reduced to 50-years. Mr. Ballbusta has emphasized to me that it would be extremely prudent for you to accept his proposition.

Please contact me with your reply before April 15, the date Mr. Ballbusta has been invited to spend time upstate with some long-term friends.

Thank you in advance,

Sincerely,

Morris Shapiro

Response:

The Devil
1548 Netherworld Ave.
Hell, 76804

Mr. Morris Shapiro
14 East 38th Street
New York City, 10018   March 29, 2005

Dear Mr. Shapiro:

Thank you for your letter regarding your client, Mr. Louis Ballbusta. Such an offer has never been proposed before. It should have been taken up by our Admission's Committee early this month, but was delayed because a member was accidentally burned while he was barbecuing and had to be hospitalized. Such accidents occur here frequently. He should be discharged soon because our "Burn Unit" has been universally accepted as the largest and best in the world by *U.S. News and World Reports*

Last Tuesday, the Committee met and your proposal created a great deal of heated discussion. In one argument, one of our members broke the legs of a particularly vociferous opponent. Furthermore, you might be surprised to learn that another of our members, who was conspicuous for his ugly prizefighter's nose and uglier crisscrossing facial scars, was actually once the victim of one of Mr. Ballbusta's temper tantrums.

In addition, a woman on our Committee, known for remunerative erogenous activities and for tainting the entire Delaware Police Force with a rare form of the clap, remembered Mr. Ballbusta from the days she worked Atlantic City. He apparently stiffed her big time. She is pressing for his admission even before he is buried, in fact, even before he has died.

The Committee was only too happy to allow you to air condition my personal facilities, but was adamantly opposed to even considering it for Mr. Ballbusta's friends. Adamantly! Although the offer was personally tempting, such temptation is a sin that our indoctrination lectures emphasizes and strongly discourages. I, therefore, believe that for the overall good of our community, that the offer must be refused. Furthermore, from some facts that The Committee has collected on Mr. Ballbusta's personal life, it was unanimously agreed that Louis' admission is a *fait accompli*. The Committee discussed ways to insure that this lowlife be confined to the remotest suburb of our inferno so as not to "contaminate" other residents. When Mr. Ballbusta is admitted, the Committee also agreed that he should be denied bathroom privileges and admission to our hilarious monthly roasts.

Furthermore, our Financial Secretary opined that the economic burden resulting from air conditioning even my facilities alone would be too onerous, because we anticipate extraordinary expenses due to construction of additional housing for the hoard of American business executives and financial big shots destined to be admitted soon.

Finally, it was unanimously agreed that an investigative sub-committee be organized to determine the suitability of admitting Mr. B's upstate friends.

Thank you for your interest in our community,

Sincerely
Lucifer

Dreams

It seems logical to me that writers dream more than ordinary people. Interesting people also probably dream more than the average Joe. Worried and troubled people, like Jews, definitely dream more than other people. Absolutely. Look it up. And why shouldn't they worry? They eat terrible foods—greasy pastrami, salty lox and Killer chocolate cakes. And what about the billion Muslims who hate them?

I can't imagine my boring neighbor, Plotkin, dreaming. He never has anything to say about anything. When I rushed over to his house a week ago to tell him that the Americans found Saddam Hussein hiding in a teeny hole in the ground, all he said was "So?" However, that talkative, loud-mouth Rabinowitz, who is always telling smutty jokes and interrupting me in mid-sentence, even one-word sentences, to tell me some cockamamie story about his job in the "Complaint Department" of Macy's, is definitely someone who dreams. I'm also sure that stutterers, like Katz, must have the same dreams, repeated night after night. Lately, I've considered the dreams of animals. I know it sounds sort of nutty, but doesn't it figure that the speechless giraffe doesn't dream, whereas those babbling and screeching, funny-looking lemurs from Madagascar, probably dream like Alice. And what about cockroaches?

I first started to dream a lot after I took my first class in creative writing. I loved the class, and, more important, my teacher liked my work. She wrote her comments on *Post-it* notes and attached them to the first page of my short stories. She was always curious about the people in my stories, using phrases such as "I'd like to know more about your character. He seems so complex." I never really meant him to be complex. I often dreamt about the stories and it surprised me how my imagination concocted outlandish twists for them.

But, then I wondered, where do dreams come from?

I imagine that the actors in dreams are housed in something like an imaginary hotel of the brain. The people who have played important roles in the dreamer's life arrive, sign the registry and take elevators to their assigned rooms. In some miraculous way, deceased people are resuscitated and checked in also, probably through a side door. Even animals important in one's life are checked in and escorted to rooms by Helmut, a well-known animal trainer, who sports a yellow windbreaker with the words "Animal Trainer" emblazoned on its back. The animals are usually well behaved and rarely bark or chirp because they are accustomed to their familiar leashes or cages that the trainer brings with him. He registers as calmly and as nonchalantly as if he was checking in with his wife. Guests may notice the animals, but management is only too happy to accommodate because someone is paying big bucks for the rooms.

Probably, the older you are, the larger the hotel and the more rooms it will contain. Relatives and friends, who play a prominent part in our everyday lives, are entitled to penthouses with stunning views and sunsets. The two guys who went with me to a burlesque house in Newark when I was a pimply teenager, and whom I really wasn't wild about, just might show up in minor roles. I think they should be given a cramped room at the end of the hall, near the noisy icemaker.

Most of my aunts and uncles are on the higher floors.

On a top floor, Stan, Sean and Bobby, high-school friends who I still see often, occupy the Presidential suite. Lipshitz, the bully, was given a crummy room with a view of a flophouse. The cop who gave me a speeding ticket for going three miles over the limit in a 70-mile-per-hour zone in upstate New York is given a tiny room in the subbasement of the hotel, near the boiler room. He really should be put *in* the boiler room.

When the participants in my dream are all in their rooms, it will be easy to rap on their doors and announce, "Ready in ten, please." A wardrobe mistress has already entered each of the player's room hours before, and brought in an assortment of clothing appropriate for the evening's dream. After ten minutes, when they have all assembled in the hall, they are escorted to the "Dream Room" where they are told the essence of the dream that night, sometimes of the "nightmare" that night. Strangers meet and greet each other and small talk can be heard before the performance begins. Some kiss and become teary eyed.

Once, "Big Dick," my buddy when we went looking for chicks at the Concord or Grossingers, seduced Lipshitz's buxom sister and disappeared for almost an hour in an adjoining closet. A waiter, carrying a tray of pigs-in-blankets, who wandered mistakenly into the Dream Room, ended up taking Big Dick's part. Also, a week ago, a bewildered housekeeper came in holding a soiled toilet plunger in her right hand and a few soggy condoms in the other. Both of the staff were offered cameo roles in future performances.

When the dream is over, everybody returns to his or her room, packs and checks out. Some participants go directly home or to work, and, surprisingly, a few take taxis or catch flights for other dreams.

The director and producer of all productions is my Freudian psychiatrist, Bruno, who I have seen for over twenty years. He is a high earner and pays for all the rooms. I once complained that I didn't think I was making any progress even though I saw him three times a week. Immediately, he responded by suggesting that I see him four times a week.

Bruno plans my dreams after my late afternoon session, scurrying from his East 70's office in a custom Masserati. As soon as Bruno arrives at the hotel, he begins preparations for the dream and then directs it. On the days when I don't see him, he oversees the production of other patient's dreams at other hotels. He does pro bono work for a few of his impoverished former patients who had seen him seven days a week when they were fat cats.

As you are reading this story, have you thought about the many people and animals all over the world who are dreaming right now? They may be getting up from a deep sleep, sitting on the side of their bed, scrunching their eyebrows and struggling to remember the dream they just had. Some may have slept fitfully because of nightmares that caused them to tremble when they awoke. The nightmares often involved wild-eyed strangers who were lunging at them with carving knives or college professors who refused them admission to take an important final exam because they arrived just a minute or two late.

Usually, people dream in bed, but one can also dream on a long train ride, on a jet to Europe or on a cross-country trip on a Greyhound bus. Most dreamers will be unable to remember anything about their dreams, although every one of them, whether they are herdsmen in Mongolia, aborigines in Australia or rabbis in Israel, will probably know that they had dreamt.

Dreams occur mainly during REM sleep and they last for a few hours, roughly the time one spends viewing all sorts of entertainment, like TV, movies or plays, except there's no need for babysitters, no travel time and no tolls. You don't have to wear your glasses or adjust your hearing aids. You're never late to a performance because of schmucks causing accidents on the expressway or have to wait on line because of bumbling old people searching for credit cards. There are no idiotic trailers or ads for the local podiatrist.

Nobody interrupts the dream opening candy wrappers or answering cell phones. You can wear anything when you dream or you can wear beans. Best of all, when you have wet dreams, you never get AIDS.

There are drawbacks. You can't munch popcorn and you can't drink a Coke. You can't walk out early or get a better seat. But, the price is right and there are no exorbitant parking fees. But, it may cost you big time for a shrink.